S0-BEB-519

Family
Secrets

Family Secrets

Barbara Corcoran

A Jean Karl Book
ATHENEUM • 1992 • NEW YORK
Maxwell Macmillan Canada
TORONTO
Maxwell Macmillan International
NEW YORK   OXFORD   SINGAPORE   SYDNEY

Atheneum
Macmillan Publishing Company
866 Third Avenue
New York, NY 10022

Maxwell Macmillan Canada, Inc.
1200 Eglinton Avenue East
Suite 200
Don Mills, Ontario M3C 3N1

Macmillan Publishing Company is part of the Maxwell Communication Group of Companies.

First Edition

Printed in the United States of America

10 9 8 7 6 5 4 3 2 1

The text of this book is set in 12½/15 Garamond #3.

Book design by Patrice Fodero

LIBRARY OF CONGRESS CATALOGING-IN-PUBLICATION DATA

Corcoran, Barbara.
        Family secrets/Barbara Corcoran. —1st ed.
            p.   cm.
        "A Jean Karl book."
        Summary: After moving with her lively family to the small town where her father grew up, thirteen-year-old Tracy discovers that she is adopted, a surprise that brings her new insights into what constitutes a family.
        ISBN 0-689-31744-1
        [1. Adoption—Fiction.   2. Family life—Fiction.]   I. Title.
        PZ7.C814Fam   1992
        [Fic]—dc20   91-13104

This book is for
Arthur and Jean Towne
and Ed Josephs,
who brought Essex vividly back to my mind

The town in this story is basically Essex, Massachusetts, but I have taken some liberties with geography and with stores and other places. The characters are entirely invented.

Chapter 1

❖   ❖   ❖

Tracy sat down on a packing box to catch her breath. Her older sister, Alison, was sprawled on the sofa where the movers had left it, in the middle of the big living room. She was listening to her Walkman.

Outdoors their father was backing the U-Haul up to the steps, the twins shouting conflicting directions.

"Little more, Dad, little more," Arnold yelled.

"Whoa, Dad! You're going to hit the steps." Cautious Richard was right; Tracy heard the thump of wheels against wood.

It had taken three days, finally, to make the move from Boston to this small North Shore town where their father had grown up. He had been talking about it for a long time, but only the twins had shared his enthusiasm.

When the subject came up, Alison always said, "Dad, you can't go home again. Everybody knows that. It won't be the same."

"It's one of the few towns I know of that's hardly changed," he always said. "Anyway, it's a good place for you kids to grow up. I won't have to worry every day about your getting mugged."

Then something happened that made a difference. He got a year's sabbatical from the history department at Radcliffe to work on the second volume of his history of New England. And even Tracy could see that there was not enough space for him to work in the old cluttered apartment they lived in on Newbury Street.

"His card files and floppy disks would fill up the place," Alison said. She was not so opposed to moving as she had been, once she found out there was a daily commuter train to Boston from nearby Beverly Farms. She could still get to town for football games and dances and plays. Alison was a senior in high school, but most of her friends were in college—Harvard and MIT and Radcliffe. Alison was beautiful and sophisticated, Tracy thought, and she wished she were just like her.

Tracy moved out of the way as her father and the twins wrestled the big TV-VCR off the truck and up the steps. The boys were excited about moving. They had been talking for days about getting a boat for the nearby river. "And fried clams!" Arnold kept saying. "We can eat our weight in fried clams."

But Tracy missed Boston already. She was used to the noise and dirt and the weirdos on the street. She loved walking in the Public Gardens on the way to her small private school. She liked the public library, where she could find books she had never dreamed existed. And the foreign movies she and her friend Kath went to. She felt uneasy about this small town on the river, and she dreaded her new school where she wouldn't know anyone.

"Watch it, Arnold," their father said as the TV scraped against the door frame.

"Not to worry, Dad. A little furniture polish and you won't even see the scars." Arnold the unflappable.

Alison stretched and took off her earphones. "What do you think of the house, Trace?"

Tracy shrugged. "Okay." In fact, she liked the house. She just didn't want to live in this town. She had an uneasy feeling about it that she couldn't explain. The house itself was nice. It certainly had plenty of room—three floors, five bedrooms, two bathrooms on the second floor and a small one on the third floor where Tracy had chosen to have her room. They wouldn't be bumping into each other all the time here and yelling for their turn at the bathroom. There was even a tiny powder room downstairs.

The house hadn't been lived in for several years, and the kitchen and the one original bathroom had been pretty primitive, but her parents had put their heads together with an architect friend, and now everything was new and convenient. The kitchen had every appliance and gadget one could think of.

Tracy got up and brought in some more boxes from the truck. When she started to put them on the floor, the top one—an old metal lockbox—fell off; the lid sprang open, and the papers inside spilled out onto the floor.

"Nice work, Sis," Alison said in her drawly voice.

"At least I'm doing something," Tracy said. She and Alison tossed remarks at each other, but they actually got along better than most of the sisters Tracy knew.

She sat on the floor to gather up the papers. Insurance papers, the children's vaccination certificates, her grandmother's death certificate, a letter many years old from the head of the Harvard history department congratulating her father on his summa cum laude. The last packet, held together by a rubber band that broke as she touched it, contained their birth certificates: Alison, born the day before Christmas seventeen years ago, the twins, born in April eleven years ago, and her father, born in this town forty-six years ago. Hers and her mother's were not there.

Her mother came in from the kitchen, her dark red hair flying in all directions, a smudge on her cheek. Wearily she sank down on the sofa beside Alison.

"I'll never, never move again. My horoscope said this was a good time for a move, but it didn't say how much work it would be. I'll say one thing, though, that kitchen is a dream. It's so big, I could use roller skates."

"Mom, how come your and my birth certificates aren't here with the others?" Tracy asked.

"Birth certificates? I keep mine in my passport case."

"Where's mine?"

"Probably in the bank with the other papers."

"What other papers?"

Before her mother had a chance to answer, Arnold burst in, staggering under a load of books. "I'm expiring from starvation," he said. He tripped, and half of the books cascaded to the floor.

"Arnold!" Alison said. "Watch it."

"I think it's time for a lunch break," their mother said, "before we all collapse. Everybody wash up, and we'll go over to the river for lunch."

"Fried clams!" Arnold yelled out the door to his father and brother. "Drop everything! Fried clams coming up!"

They all went upstairs to wash except Tracy, who paused to put the papers back in the box, and Alison, who stood up and stretched, watching her sister.

"Don't worry," she said, "you've got a birth certificate. I mean, obviously you were born. It's funny, though, I was three years old—old enough that I should remember things like Mom being pregnant—but I don't. I just remember that all of a sudden I had a baby sister." She laughed at Tracy's startled look. "Maybe the elves brought you. If it had been a stork, I'd have remembered." She stretched again, arching her back, and went slowly upstairs.

"Maybe they found me on the doorstep," Tracy said.

"Maybe you're a changeling." Alison disappeared toward her room.

A changeling, Tracy thought. Wasn't that a baby that got swapped for another one? She'd wondered before at how little she resembled the rest of the family. They were all blond, except for her mother, the redhead. Tracy's hair was dark brown and straight, and her eyes were what her mother called amber. Her mother's eyes were green, and the others' were blue.

Oh, well, genes did odd things. She'd learned that much in science class. Anyway, she'd read somewhere that many girls go through a spell of thinking they're adopted. She didn't really think anything like that, and in fact it was kind of fun to look different from the rest of the family. She put the box on the sofa and went up to the third floor to the odd-shaped small room with its sloping ceiling and the dormer windows that opened out toward the sea. She couldn't actually make out the ocean from here, but far across the tawny marshes was a place where the light looked different, and there, she knew, was where the sea began.

It was odd how familiar everything seemed to her, as if she had lived here in some other life. Only that was the kind of thing her mother believed in, but Tracy didn't.

"Hurry up, Trace," Arnold called up from downstairs.

And she realized she was very hungry.

6

Chapter 2

❖   ❖   ❖

As they walked along the tree-shaded street, their father eagerly pointed out familiar places. He had changed to blue sailcloth pants and a white sweater, his curly blond hair wet from the shower. He looked, Tracy thought, almost like the boy he had been in this town.

"That's Piggy Newton's house," he said. "His mother made the best pies in town."

"Figures," Alison said. "A kid doesn't get called Piggy for nothing."

"They've torn down the old Forbes house. I had a lot of good times in that place. Eight kids they had."

Arnold gave Richard a familiar signal; Richard stooped, and Arnold leapfrogged over him. Lately they had refused to dress alike, but today they were wearing matching dark green shorts and yellow T-shirts that read LISTEN TO THE KIDS.

"Do you know," Alison said, "this town has only one main street?"

"Saves buying a map," Richard said.

The restaurant they were heading for was just across the causeway that bridged the salt river. Half a dozen restaurants and clam take-out places were strung along the road, and already in June the tourist traffic was fairly heavy.

Their father pointed to a fried clam place up the street. "I used to shuck clams there after school."

"That must have been pure delight," Alison said.

"Alison, dear, try to be pleasant," her mother said.

"Mommie, dearest, this is as pleasant as I get." Alison made a crazy face, with a wide idiotic grin.

"Watch the cars," their mother called to the twins, but they had already dashed across the road in front of a slow-moving Buick. The road was too narrow for fast traffic.

Alison sauntered across in front of a convertible, smiling graciously at the good-looking young driver. Tracy watched her, amused. Alison was growing up. All their lives they had been close, but now sometimes Alison seemed a whole generation ahead. Tracy liked watching her, but she missed the old Alison who had been up to any kind of prank. Now she dated college men, talked a different language, even liked different music. Three years suddenly became a big gap.

Even the twins were changing. Richard seemed to be growing up faster than Arnold. Sometimes he showed signs of wanting to get off on his own for a few hours, but Arnold was always right behind him.

They stopped a moment in the parking lot to look at the boats moving slowly up and down the river, most of them driven by sunburned sportfishermen, probably from the city, either going out for some fishing or coming back, looking happy on their high decks. Some of them waved.

A little way upstream a colorful collection of small boats were moored off the marina.

An old outboard chugged into a small dock just below them. A boy, about seventeen or eighteen, jumped onto the dock and tied up his boat, then ran up the steep slope, passing close by them. He waved in greeting as Tracy's father called out a cheerful hello.

"Do you know him, Dad?" Alison asked.

"Never saw him before. This is a town where you speak to people."

"Wow!" Alison watched him run down the street. "Maybe this is going to be more interesting than I thought. That was what I would call a babe."

Their father leaned on the railing of the fence that enclosed the parking lot. "Smell that good salt air!"

"Where were the shipyards, Dad?" Richard asked.

"All along this shore. This was the first town in America to build ships, you know."

They knew; he had told them hundreds of times. But the boys liked to hear it.

"My father used to take me to launchings. Boy, that was a thrill! Sometimes those big old boats would tip, coming off the ways, and get stuck in the mud. The tide had to be just right or they'd just slide into the river and sink to the bottom. Story's yard, that was one of the big ones. I liked to see a ship being built, guys swarming all over, hammering and scraping, the finish men coming in at the last, and the caulkers in their smoky little shed smelling of tar."

"What's a caulker?" Richard asked.

"Fellow that took a ball of oakum and worked it into strands of rope. It was an art."

"Before Richard asks you what oakum is," his wife said, "shall we go in and order lunch?"

Tracy walked along with her father. "What *is* oakum?"

"Hemp." He opened the restaurant door and breathed deeply. "Smell those clams!"

A waitress found them a booth overlooking the river. Arnold slid into a seat by the window.

"Arnold," his father said, "ever hear of ladies first?"

"Dad," Arnold said, "that's sexist. Equal opportunity, right?" He started to move out, but Alison moved in beside him.

"Stay where you are, piggy." She rumpled his thick blond hair. "You need a haircut."

The busy waitress left menus. Tracy liked clams all right, but she was mad for lobster. She knew right away what she wanted: a lobster boiled in the shell, with melted butter. When the waitress came back, only Richard hadn't decided.

"Make up your mind, Rich," his father said. "The lady can't stand there all day."

Richard looked at the waitress with his serious frown. "I'd like a hamburger, please, hold the onions."

"Hamburger!" His father was shocked. "This is shellfish country, boy."

The waitress smiled. "Boys like their hamburgers. Well-done or medium, honey?"

"Well." He gave her his rare smile. "And french fries."

His father groaned. "Right out of McDonald's."

"Are you boys twins?" the waitress said.

"I'm the oldest," Arnold said. "Seventeen minutes."

She laughed. "I'll bring your beverages right away."

"It must be gruesome to be a waitress," Alison said when she had hurried away. "Having to be pleasant to boring people."

"Nobody in this booth is boring," Arnold said.

A teenage girl, long and lanky, with a mop of dark hair carelessly caught back in a ponytail, came along to clear dirty dishes from the booth next to theirs. She wore a long skirt and a black T-shirt with a large clam on the front. She paused and looked at them with open curiosity.

"Greetings." Dangerously, she balanced two full trays, one on top of the other. "Welcome to the home of the clam. Where you from?" She released one hand to push back her hair and almost lost control of the top tray.

Richard, sitting nearest to her, kept an anxious eye on the tray.

"We're residents," their mother said, "as of to-day."

"Wow! What humongous luck!" She looked at Alison. "You'll be going to Regional High, right?"

"Right."

"Fantastic! Senior?"

"Yes."

"I'm third year myself, but we'll ride the bus together. I predict we'll be bosom friends. You guys twins or what?"

"Or what," Arnold said.

"Ha. Very humorous." She looked at Tracy. "I can see you're a family friend. You don't look like the others."

"She's our sister," Alison said.

"Oh. Well, we can't all be peas in a pod."

Somewhere a voice called, "Rosie!"

She frowned. "My name is Dusty Rose, but some ignorant people call me Rosie. I've been a Rose of some kind in all my incarnations. Last time I was Rosemary."

"That's for rue," Tracy's father said, smiling.

The girl looked blank. "Pardon?"

Tracy's mother looked at the girl with new inter-est. "Did you say incarnations?"

"You bet. Five that I remember. Don't laugh."

"She won't laugh," Alison said. "She's a true be-liever."

"Fantastic!" Rosie said.

The waitress came up behind the girl. "Beat it, Rosie. You're holding everything up."

"*So* sorry." She thrust her right hand at Richard. "Welcome aboard."

Startled, Richard lifted his hand as a half-full glass of water slid off the tray and dumped its contents in his lap. He jumped, and the glass fell to the floor with a thud.

"Rosie!" the waitress said. "Look what you've done!"

"Not to worry. It's only plastic." She grabbed a paper napkin and tried to mop the water off Richard's lap.

"It's okay, really." Embarrassed, he took the napkin, then reached out quickly to keep the rest of the dishes on the tray from falling on him.

"Rosie, if you don't beat it right now, you're fired. I mean it."

"Alice, I'm going. Really, you shouldn't get so worked up. It's bad for your blood pressure. See you folks around." She gave them a broad smile and walked away, swinging her hips and stopping to greet several people in other booths.

"Honey, I'm sorry," the waitress said to Richard. "Are you soaked?"

"No, I'm fine, really."

"Rosie is a good kid, and someday we may get her tamed down. I'll be right back with your dinners."

When she had gone, Alison said, "Well, it's different, Dad. I'll say that for your hometown."

"Be nice to everybody; they may be one of your cousins. Half the town is related to the other half."

"That's statistically impossible," Richard said. "By the law of averages—"

"In this town the law of averages doesn't apply."

While they waited for their dinners, Tracy looked around at the other people in the restaurant. She liked the idea of being related to a lot of people. It made her feel kind of protected. Maybe it would turn out to be nice here.

Chapter 3

❖ ❖ ❖

When they had almost finished their desserts, a large man in jeans and a blue denim shirt came to the table. "Say!" he said in a booming voice. "If you're not Jackie Stewart, I'm a hornswoggled catfish!"

Tracy's father half stood, holding out his hand. "Horace!"

Horace gave him a hearty hug and said to the others, "Went to school with this boy. What he could do with a basketball! Used to take him clammin' and he didn't know one end of a clam from another, always had his nose in a goldarned book. Jackie, you old son of a seacook, what are you doin' out here in the wilds?"

"Just became a local, as of today. We moved into the old Burnett house." He introduced the man to the rest of the family, and they all got hearty handshakes.

"Came back to us, did you? Say, that's all right! You still teaching at that female seminary?"

Tracy's father laughed. "Don't let any Radcliffe

woman hear you call it that. Yep, I'm still there. On sabbatical this year to write a book."

"I read your first one. Didn't understand it, of course, too deep for me, but I told everybody the author was my old pal. Dry as dust, wasn't it?" He winked at the twins. "Listen, let's get together soon."

"You bet, Horace. That's what I'm here for."

When Horace had gone, Alison said, "Colorful type, Dad."

"Listen," her father said, "don't you put down Horace Webster. He's the salt of the earth. And he may put on that hick act, but he graduated from BU with honors, and he owns half the real estate on Cape Ann." He turned to his wife. "Horace was always sweet on Felicia. Used to serenade her under her bedroom window with his banjo till the night she dumped a pan of cold water on him." He smiled and shook his head. "He never married."

"Who's Felicia?" Alison asked.

But her father didn't answer; he was busy getting out his wallet and figuring the tip.

"Little Jackie Stewart," Arnold said to his twin. "Basketball."

Richard shook his head. "Children are the last to know."

They all went outside while their father settled the bill. They were probably going to learn lots of things about their father, Tracy thought, now that they were in his home territory. It was strange to think about your parents having been kids, maybe having had the same kind of problems you had.

As they were standing outside, a siren went off, rising and moaning and rising. Several people, including their waitress and the girl called Rosie, rushed to the door as a fire engine came along the causeway and cars pulled off the road. The boy who had passed them in the parking lot, the one Alison had said was a babe, came racing down the road, and as the fire engine had to slow for a car ahead, he swung onto the back of the fire truck, pulled aboard by the firemen.

"There goes Davey," Rosie said to the waitress. "Gives him a scare."

"Don't gossip about things you don't know for sure," the waitress said.

"Are fires so rare here?" Tracy's mother said to the waitress. "We get those screaming sirens all the time in Boston."

It was Rosie who answered. "We think there's a firebug," she said.

"Hush up, Rosie," the waitress said.

A man standing near them said, "Well, that last fire was set for sure."

"I thought this town was dead as a dinosaur," Arnold said.

The man laughed. "We have our moments."

Tracy felt a chill. A firebug didn't sound like a very safe person to have around. Some of these old houses, like the one they lived in, would go up like a torch.

Her mother took her hand and they crossed the road. "I guess there are problems everywhere," she said. She smiled at Tracy. "Even here in your dad's paradise." As they reached the other side of the road, she said, "Do you think you're going to like it here, Tracy?"

"Mom, how can I tell? We've just got here." Then as her mother looked worried, she said, "I probably will. I'm slow getting used to new things."

Her mother was silent for a minute. "Your dad and I want to have a talk with you later, perhaps tonight. There's something important we want to tell you."

Tracy felt a shiver of foreboding. "Something bad?"

"No, no. I think you may find it quite interesting."

But Tracy felt uneasy. She didn't want to hear whatever it was. She thought about it the rest of the afternoon, while she was unpacking. She didn't like surprises, and some nervousness in her mother's voice made her think she was *not* going to find it interesting. *Interesting* was the word her parents used about people or books or whatever, when they didn't want to be rude enough to say they didn't like it.

Whatever it is, she thought, I'm not going to like it.

Chapter 4

❖ ❖ ❖

By the time her mother asked her to come into her father's study, Tracy was really nervous. When teachers and parents and grown-ups in general said they wanted to "have a little talk," it usually turned out that you'd done something wrong. Maybe she hadn't worked hard enough on the moving. Or maybe they wanted her to improve her attitude toward their new home.

Alison had gone up to her room, and the twins were outside, rigging up a swing with an old tire hanging from one of the big trees. She felt deserted.

Her father's study was still a jumble of unshelved books, but his computer was set up. He was sitting the wrong way around on his office chair, his arms braced on the back. Her mother sat on the edge of the big leather chair. Both of them looked anxious. Maybe they were going to send her off to boarding school. Much as the idea of public school scared her, a boarding school loomed in her mind like the greatest horror, like being banished to Siberia. Some of her friends had gone to boarding school and hated it.

"What's up?" She tried to sound cool, like Alison.

"Sit down, dear," her mother said, "if you can find a place."

Tracy perched on a box of books. She hoped this wasn't going to last long. She looked at her parents. They looked at each other.

Her mother gave a nervous little laugh and said, "We've rehearsed this so often, I thought I had my lines down pat, but now I can't think . . ."

"Lines?" Tracy frowned. "Is this doomsday or what? Are you going to tell me I'm a changeling or something?"

Her mother gave a little gasp. "Changeling? Whatever made you think of such a thing? No, darling, you're no changeling." She reached over and caught Tracy's hand in a hard squeeze.

Maybe her mother had cancer! Frightened, she tried to think if she had noticed any symptoms.

"We're keeping you in suspense," her father said, "and that's exactly what we didn't mean to do." His voice was gentle. "It isn't anything bad, Trace. It's just going to surprise you. Let me begin at the beginning." He took out his cigarette case, opened it, and put it back in his pocket. He had stopped smoking last New Year's Day. The case was empty. "A classmate and friend of mine from here left town right after gradua- tion. She was the kind of girl all the boys fall for, but

20

I happened not to, so she trusted me as a friend, and we kept in touch in a haphazard sort of way."

"She came to the apartment one day, before you were born," her mother said, "so I got to know her. She was very beautiful."

Tracy listened, puzzled. What did this have to do with her?

"She was a singer, sort of folk song and women's song—"

"Kind of like Joan Baez," her mother said.

Her father smiled. "Only not as successful. Anyway, let me see if I can't shorten this: She got married to a sort of artist who hung around just long enough to get her pregnant and then disappeared."

"Without knowing she was pregnant, to do him justice." Her mother was still holding her hand in a tight grip.

"She didn't feel she could take care of a baby, living so much on the road and all that, so she asked us to adopt the child." He paused.

An idea was beginning to form in Tracy's mind, an idea she didn't want to face.

"So?" She realized that she sounded angry.

"So we were the winners," her mother said. She got up and put her arms around Tracy. "You were that baby, and our lives have been richer than I can tell you because of you."

Tracy felt as if she had touched an electric wire. She jerked away from her mother. "So now you tell me.

Haven't you ever heard that adopted kids should be told early? Why do you spring it on me now?"

"We know how you feel," her father said, "but—"

"You couldn't possibly know how I feel. You're not even related to me. Alison and the twins are not my sister and brothers. . . ." Her voice broke.

"Tracy—"

Her mother interrupted him. "Let her be angry, Jack. She's entitled."

"But I must explain, Tracy. We signed a legal document that said we were not to tell you, or anyone, until either you were eighteen or your birth mother died."

"Believe us, we wanted to tell you," her mother said. "We longed to tell you."

"I'm not eighteen . . . ," Tracy began, and stopped.

"Your mother died, a few days before we moved here. She knew we were making the move, and she wrote us that she was dying of lung cancer. The phone call and the follow-up letter from her lawyer released us from our agreement."

"We waited a few days," her mother said, "to give us all a chance to settle down here."

"Have a kid, but don't let her get in your way. Sounds like a real great mother. What was her name?"

"Felicia Shaw."

"Real name or singing name?"

"Her real name. We don't know your father's name."

"They sound like real stable parents."

"Tracy," her mother said softly, "we are your parents."

"In every sense of the word," her father said, "except the actual birth." He stood up and hugged her.

"Wow. I've got a really great background, haven't I?"

"We've tried to give you a happy background. Tracy, it's our family you belong to." Her mother looked pleading.

"Well, I can't paint, and I can't carry a tune."

"You look like Felicia," her father said. "She was a beautiful and charming woman."

"I suppose everybody knows about this but me? Alison and the twins and this whole town?"

"Nobody knows it," her father said, "and there's no reason anyone needs to know it unless you want them to."

"I think I'll go lie down."

When she was at the door, her mother said, "Tracy? We love you with all our hearts. Just as much as we love the other children."

"Yeah. Well . . ." Tracy took a deep breath. "I guess it's not you I'm angry at. I mean, if you couldn't help not telling me. It's just kind of a shock." She bit her lip as tears stung her eyes. She went out and ran upstairs to her room.

She threw herself on the bed and stared at the ceiling. It was a strange ceiling, with little shiny dots here and there, like stars.

She wondered what her mother had been like. Probably sang in some dive, getting high every night, boozing it up all day. Well, so long, Mother, it was nice not knowing you. She picked up Paddington Bear, who was always on her bed, and threw him as hard as she could at the wall.

Then she got up and brought him back to the bed. "Poor old Paddington. It's not your fault."

So Alison was not her sister, and the twins were not related to her. "I am a stranger and alone." Wasn't that from some poem?

She hugged Paddington tight. "If anybody thinks I'm up here crying my eyes out, they're wrong. I'm just mad, that's all. Grown-ups are supposed to have some sense of responsibility, aren't they? Okay, lesson number one: They don't."

Chapter 5

❖　❖　❖

She timed her arrival downstairs the next day. She knew Alison would sleep another hour at least, and she had heard the twins go out. The car had gone off too, so at least one parent—and maybe both—had gone out.

But her mother was in the kitchen, still putting dishes on the shelves and unpacking cooking things. She smiled at Tracy anxiously.

"Good morning, honey. I made some of those bran-and-date muffins you like. Do you feel like eggs?"

"No, thanks." Tracy felt sorry for her. She wanted to act natural and to tell her mother—her *adopted* mother—to relax. But she couldn't relax herself.

They made polite conversation, like two strangers, about the woman next door who had come over and introduced herself.

"She seems very nice. Mrs. Keenan, her name is. She has a boy about the twins' age."

"That's nice," Tracy said.

"Your father has gone to look at boats. I think the boys went with him. He wants a good secondhand rowboat with an outboard motor. I don't know a blessed thing about boats, but of course he does."

Tracy looked at her mother, thinking about her childhood in North Carolina. "Do you ever get homesick for the South?"

Her mother looked up quickly. "I used to, a lot. I guess I still do, but after your grandparents died, I didn't want to go back there anymore."

"They weren't my grandparents, Mom," Tracy said gently.

Her mother flushed. "Technically, no, they weren't. But they always thought of you as a beloved grandchild."

Tracy hardly remembered them, but she didn't say so.

"Tracy, you don't hold it against us, do you?"

"Mom, of course not. I just have to get used to it."

"I know. I know." Her mother leaned against the sink, looking out the window. "I always hated that part about not telling you. It seemed deceitful."

"It wasn't your fault." She finished her muffin and drank her milk. "I guess I'll go for a walk. See what this town is like." At the door she said, "I suppose everybody will look at me and wonder how come I look just like Felicia Shaw?"

"Oh, I don't think so. Felicia left here right after she got out of high school. We saw her a few times when she was living in Boston, but I don't think she ever came back here. She didn't like this town."

"Is this town full of her family?"

"She didn't have any family, except one cousin she used to write to. Her parents had died."

Tracy thought of something else just as she was going out. "She's the one who dumped the water on Horace what's-his-name?"

"Yes. He was really mad about her, I guess."

Tracy laughed. "Well, she had some spirit anyway. See you later, Mom."

She walked up the street, returning the wave of the woman who was probably Mrs. Keenan, out trimming her hedge. She had had a hard time sleeping, and she felt numb today, emotions all washed out. You get up in the morning one person, and you go to bed somebody else. It was hard to know how to react to it, but she'd probably get used to it. She didn't know yet whether she wanted to tell Alison and the boys. Sooner or later probably.

At a phone booth near the restaurant she looked up Shaw in the phone book, but there weren't any. She wondered what her father's name was. He probably wasn't from around here, anyway. A painter. Probably one of those "artists" who painted garish scenes on fake velvet and sold them to cheap souvenir shops.

She sat on a bench overlooking the river. The tide was out, and three clam diggers were working on the flats below her, stooped over and digging their three-tined forks into the mud, scooping clams into slatted wooden baskets. They wore hip-high rubber boots and hats pulled down over their eyes.

"Takin' in the sights?" The loud voice behind her made her jump. "Remember me? Dusty Rose. We met yesterday noon."

"Oh, hi," Tracy said.

Rosie sat down beside her. She was wearing white shorts rolled high on her long, tanned legs and a purple tank top. "I don't go on duty till five today." She stretched.

"Do you ever go clamming?"

"No, you have to have a license so the river won't get clammed out. Anyway, it's hard work, worse than hustling trays."

Tracy tried to think of something else to say. She really didn't feel like making conversation. "Where was the fire yesterday?"

"It was just an old shack over to South Essex. No great loss. They think it was set."

"Is there really somebody around here who sets fires?"

"Seems to be. Might be kids, might not. I have my ideas." She looked mysterious. "Well, they'll catch him sooner or later. Firebugs always go back to watch the place burn. They can't help it." She jumped up. "Got to get home and fix my mother's lunch. See you around. What'd you say your name is?"

"Tracy."

"See you, Trace." She ran across the road and up a side street.

Tracy wondered why Rosie had to fix her mother's lunch. Was her mother sick? She got up and half climbed, half slid down the embankment to the flats. The mud was squishy. She kept close to the shore and made her way to a big boulder that looked like a good place to sit. She needed to sort out how she really felt about this adoption thing. It would have been better if her parents could have told her a long time ago; then it wouldn't have been so hard to get used to. Was this Felicia Shaw afraid Tracy would show up and ruin her career or something? She sounded like a flake.

One of the clam diggers waded out to his boat, loaded his clams in the bow, pulled up the anchor, and rowed away. One of the others moved farther along the shore.

Tracy noticed that the one nearest her was a woman; a tall, broad-shouldered woman, quite old, dressed like the others in faded jeans and high boots and, in her case, a wide-brimmed straw hat.

The woman straightened carefully, her hand on the small of her back. She noticed Tracy and said, "Howdy." Her gray eyes, set in a long, tanned face, were the kind that looked directly at you.

"Hello," Tracy said.

The woman leaned back a little and winced. "I swear this is my last summer clamming. Maybe my last day. No sense keeping at it till I can't stand up."

"It looks hard."

"What they say around here is, to be a clammer

you need a strong back and a weak mind. All right if I share your rock for a minute?"

"Sure. It's not my rock." Tracy made room for her.

The woman sat down slowly, bracing herself with one hand on the rock. "My name's Esther Story." She held out her hand.

"I'm Tracy Stewart." She liked the strong way the woman shook hands.

"Summer visitor?"

"No, we just moved here. My father grew up here."

"Which Stewart would that be?"

"John."

Miss Story's face lit up. "Young Jackie Stewart! I had him in the eighth grade. Very bright lad."

"Oh, you're a teacher?" She tried to imagine her father in the eighth grade.

"Retired. I threw in the towel after forty-six years. Your father teaches at Vassar or Wellesley, doesn't he?"

"Radcliffe. He taught one year at Vassar a long time ago. He's on a year's sabbatical now to write a book."

"More New England history?"

"Yes. Second volume."

"I read the first one. Good scholarly job. Well. I'll look forward to seeing him."

"Do you remember all your students?"

"Only the interesting ones. From Jack's class there was Horace Webster—"

"We met him last night."

"A good boy, Horace is. Let's see, Muriel Swan, married that fellow over to Newburyport; Harrison Sams, killed in Vietnam; Felicia Shaw—"

"What was she like?"

"Felicia? A beautiful oddball, always a little out of control. Went through her life like a shooting star that lost its orbit. If shooting stars have orbits. I guess they don't, do they? Well, I'd better get along before I talk you to death." She started to get up, but her back made a faint cracking sound, and she sat down quickly, her face tight with pain. "Blast! There goes the ball game." She sucked in her breath. "Tracy, see if you can catch that fellow in the blue shirt, just pulling anchor. Ask him if he'll get me into my boat and give me a tow home. His name is Wendell."

Tracy jumped off the rock and ran toward the boat, but the man was facing away from her, starting his outboard. "Mister!" she shouted. "Mister Wendell." But he didn't hear her, and the boat chugged slowly away.

Tracy ran back to Miss Story. "He didn't hear me. But I can row a boat. I'll help you get in and take you home."

"I live on an island. And I'm no lightweight."

"I'm pretty strong. I can call my father later to come and get me. He's buying a boat today." She really wanted to help Miss Story. It was interesting to think she'd been not only her father's teacher but Felicia Shaw's as well.

31

Tracy picked up the basket heaped with clams and half carried, half dragged it to the boat, splashing through the cold water that came halfway to her knees. Getting the basket into the boat wasn't easy—the thing was heavier than it looked—but she got her knee under it and hoisted it over the side. Mud oozed into her sneakers.

"Well done," Miss Story said. "Now. Getting me up isn't any lead-pipe cinch, and you be careful you don't strain *your* back." She hooked one arm around Tracy's neck. "We'll give it the old college try." She braced her other hand on the rock and said, "Heave!"

She was on her feet, breathing hard, her mouth tight with pain. "Slow and easy does it."

Tracy had strong arm and shoulder muscles from swimming. It would be easier if she were taller, but there was no help for that. Very slowly, being careful not to slip in the mud, she got to the boat. She held the stern end down as low as she could to get Miss Story over the gunwale into the stern seat.

As soon as she had the anchor stowed under the bow, she put one foot in the boat and pushed off with the other. Fitting the oars into the oarlocks, she pulled the boat around.

"It's not far," Miss Story said. "Head for the channel, out there in the middle, and then pull to your right." After a minute she said, "Doing fine. Bear to the left just a mite. Got some rocks in here."

Tracy enjoyed rowing. She hadn't been in a boat

since the summers they used to spend in New Hampshire.

When they came to the big, rocky island, Miss Story directed her alongshore to her own dock. Tracy brought the boat in smoothly and scrambled out to tie it up.

Getting Miss Story out wasn't easy, but they managed it finally. Another boat with an outboard motor was tied up on the far side of the dock.

"Leave the clams," Miss Story said. "David can look after them when he comes by."

Tracy wondered if that was the same David they had seen jumping onto the fire truck. But getting Miss Story up the path to her door left her no breath to ask questions. She just hoped Miss Story wasn't going to pass out from the pain.

When they got to the screened-in porch, Miss Story said, "Set me down on the couch, please."

Tracy braced the door with her knee and maneuvered Miss Story onto the couch. Miss Story leaned back against the solid pillows and gradually got her legs up onto the couch. She blew her breath out through pursed lips. "We made it." She looked pale.

"Can I get you some aspirin or something?" Tracy took a colorful afghan from the back of the couch and laid it gently over Miss Story's legs.

"Kitchen cabinet over the sink. Not aspirin, Anaprox, prescrip."

Tracy went into the house. It was a pleasant, comfortable-looking place, simply furnished, with a big framed painting of a clipper ship on one wall. The east wall had two wide windows facing toward the ocean.

In the tidy little kitchen she found the Anaprox, filled a glass with water, and brought them to Miss Story.

Miss Story nodded her thanks and took one of the capsules. She sighed. "You must be some kind of guardian angel, sitting there on that old rock just when I needed you."

"I'm glad I was there. If you don't mind, I'll stay a little while and fix you some lunch when you feel like it."

Miss Story sighed. "Nice. One other thing—heating pad on the table beside my bed."

Tracy loved the bedroom with its big four-poster and bright braided rugs. Several colorful afghans, one partly finished, were folded neatly on a sea chest. She brought the heating pad to the porch and found the outlet to plug it in. Then she eased Miss Story's muddy boots off.

"Florence Nightingale," Miss Story murmured. "I'll probably doze off from the Anaprox. Make yourself at home. Blueberry pie in the cupboard. Iced tea in the fridge. Whatever. Help yourself." She closed her eyes.

Tracy took Miss Story's boots and her own wet sneakers to the little patio in back of the house and set them in the sun. She hosed the mud off and left them to dry. Miss Story's small garden, hedged in against the wind, was bright with hollyhocks up against the gray-shingled house, and geraniums, dianthus, petunias, and other flowers she didn't recognize in neat rows. It would be a nice place to live if you didn't mind getting stranded here in bad weather.

In the kitchen she cut herself a piece of pie, poured some iced tea, and went back to sit on the sunny steps. She felt relaxed for the first time since they had moved to this town.

Chapter 6

❖   ❖   ❖

While Miss Story slept, Tracy looked around to see
what she could fix her for lunch. She decided on a tuna
fish sandwich with a little chopped onion and some
mayonnaise, the way Tracy herself liked it. The tuna
fish was from one of the companies that were careful
about dolphins.

She sliced a tomato, wrapped everything in foil,
and put it in the refrigerator. If Miss Story wasn't in a
tuna mood, there seemed to be enough in the refrigerator to make her something else.

In the living room Tracy looked at the rows and
rows of books on the built-in shelves: histories, bio-
graphies, Thackeray, Jane Austen, Dickens, a lot of
poetry, crossword puzzle books and double acrostics,
cookbooks of different nationalities, and lots of mysteries. If you were an old lady and didn't want to run
around a lot, this would be a perfect house to live in.

On a bottom shelf she found a stack of yearbooks

from the days when the town had had its own high school. She wasn't sure what year her father had graduated, but she took a guess and pulled out 1965. No Jackie Stewart. She tried 1964, and sure enough, there he was, John Harrison Stewart, looking very young and serious, blond hair carefully slicked down, tie neatly tied, jacket buttoned. She studied it, trying to imagine him like that, and wishing with all her heart that that nice-looking boy had grown up to be her real father.

In the informal snapshots she found him again, making a jump shot on the basketball court. The caption said: "Jumping Jackie Stewart does it again! Whether on the court or hitting the books, our Jackie is a winner. Just ask the girls! We predict he'll be head of a big publishing house or editor in chief of a newspaper."

Jumping Jackie. He never had talked about being a basketball star. The twins would like to hear that name. She glanced through the pictures of the girls, wondering which ones had fallen for him. She held her breath when she came to the *S*s; now she would see what Felicia Shaw looked like. But there was no picture of her, nothing except her name listed on the page of graduates. What a disappointment! What was the matter with Felicia anyway? Was she too irresponsible to show up at picture-taking time? Tracy was suddenly so angry with this woman who had been her mother, she felt like throwing the yearbook across the room. If it hadn't been for the Stewarts, she could have ended up in an orphanage or a foster home or out on the street.

She thought about street kids she had seen in Boston, hanging out in alleys, scrounging through garbage cans, ducking the cops. They probably had had mothers who didn't want them.

She put the book back on the shelf and looked at the framed photographs on the drop-leaf table. One was a man and woman dressed in old-fashioned clothes, probably Miss Story's parents. They looked nice. One was an enlarged snapshot of a youngish man and woman, a pretty girl about twelve or thirteen, and a boy who was certainly the babe named David, taken maybe a couple of years ago. So lucky David had his own family, and they looked good. The man and woman, dressed in shorts and T-shirts, were smiling at the children, and the girl, in a swimsuit, hair rumpled, was grinning. David was in swim trunks too, and you could see a beach in the background. So the David that Miss Story had mentioned must be *the* David, and it looked as if he was related to her. Well, her dad had said everybody in this town was related to everybody else, one way or another. If this David took Tracy back to shore, Alison would be green with jealousy.

Tracy looked through the window to see if Miss Story was still asleep and noticed that the sky was clouding up, really dark clouds in the east. Maybe a thunderstorm coming.

The sound of an outboard caught her attention. A boat was coming around the bend heading for Miss Story's dock. Whoever it was, he was coming in so fast that it looked as if he would crash into the dock, but at the last minute he reversed, shut off the motor, and glided in smoothly.

He got out, tied the lines, and glanced up at the cottage. It looked like David, but Tracy wasn't sure. He was wearing faded cutoffs, a khaki shirt with the sleeves cut off at the shoulders, sunglasses, and an old beat-up yachting cap, and he was barefoot. He leaned down and lifted Miss Story's basket of clams into his own boat.

It was okay if it was David, but what if it was somebody else stealing Miss Story's clams? Tracy decided she had better find out.

When she reached the dock, he had his back to her, bending over Miss Story's boat.

"Those are Miss Story's clams," she said.

He jumped, then turned his head without straightening up. "So?"

"Well, I mean, you can't just take them. Unless you're David."

He straightened up and looked at her, his hands on his hips. "David who?"

That confused her. Was it David, being funny, or was it somebody else? He looked tough, standing like that.

"David that Miss Story knows."

He gave her a long stare. "Do I know you?"

"No."

"Well, we better go see if I'm the David Miss Story knows." He strode up the path to the cottage.

It's David, she thought, and he's making fun of

me. Well, ha-ha, very funny, I don't think. She followed right behind him.

Miss Story was just waking up.

"Hi, Aunt Es," he said. "What are you doing laid out like that? We're going to have a thunderstorm."

"Is there some connection between those two sentences?" Miss Story said. "Hello, David. This is Tracy Stewart. Tracy, this is my nephew, David Haskell."

David took off his sunglasses and grinned. "She thought I was a clam thief."

"You could have told me," Tracy said.

"Always keep 'em guessin'. Aunt Es, why the heating pad? Back problems?"

"You could say that. I went clamming—"

"I've *told* you—"

"—and I got transfixed, you might say, like the mermaid on the rock. Couldn't move. Tracy here came to the rescue. If you ever need an instant medic, I recommend her."

"I'll bear it in mind. But you know better than to go clamming."

"I paid for my license. Hate to waste that money."

"So you'll pay twice that much to the doctor."

"Nonsense. I can take care of it myself." She looked at the sky. "Why don't you get me into my bed and take off before that storm hits? I told Tracy you'd give her a lift to shore."

"I guess I can manage it." He bent down and helped Miss Story to her feet.

Tracy followed them into the bedroom. As if he

had done it often before, David found her two canes and leaned them against the wall where she could reach them. Then he gave her the remote for the small TV on her bureau.

"I fixed you some lunch," Tracy said. "Shall I bring it in here?"

"Great," Miss Story said. "Davey, bring me the heating pad, will you?"

When they had her settled, Miss Story said, "I made a blueberry pie, but it'll keep." Thunder rolled in the distance. "You kids get going. And, Tracy, come back anytime. Thanks so much."

"Can I come tomorrow?" Tracy said. "In case you still don't feel good?"

"Love to have you. Fix it with Davey to run you over here."

Thunder crashed closer, and the rain started.

"Go, go, go." Miss Story seemed nervous.

David gave her a quick pat. "It's only here to shore," he said, more gently than he had spoken before. "Take it easy."

On their way out he grabbed a blue raincoat from the closet and gave it to Tracy. "You can bring it back tomorrow."

They ran for the boat, and as David steered it around the end of the island, the rain was pouring down and the water was beginning to rough up. Tracy held the raincoat over her head and around her shoulders.

David was getting soaked, but he didn't seem to

pay any attention. His dark glasses were in his pocket and his cap was pushed back on his head as he strained forward to see through the sheets of rain. Both he and Miss Story had seemed tense about the storm. Probably it wasn't too safe to be on the water with lightning striking all around, but she didn't feel scared.

He brought the boat ashore at a dock that apparently belonged to the motel just above it.

Shouting over the rain he said, "My house is closer. Better hole up there till the storm lets up."

She wanted to say she didn't mind going home through the rain, but he was already running up the path past the motel and across the road.

Lightning hit nearby with a smash of thunder just as David led the way to his house. It was a neat-looking Cape Cod house with dormer windows on the second floor.

"Make yourself at home." He pointed to the living room at the left of the hall as he disappeared. A few minutes later he came back wearing dry jeans and a sweater, and tossed a gray sweatshirt at Tracy. She assumed it was his, but it was small enough to fit her. Maybe his sister's, that girl in the picture at Miss Story's.

He piled kindling and two small logs on the fireplace and lit the kindling. "Get warm. I'll rustle up some coffee. You old enough to drink coffee?"

"Of course," she said, although at home she wasn't allowed to.

He disappeared again. She looked around the room and decided she liked it. The furniture was old—some of it she thought was antique—but it was a comfortable room. On a piano in the corner there was a picture of David and his family, like the one at Miss Story's. She wondered where his mother was, and his sister.

When he came back with the coffee, she said, "Isn't your mother here?"

He gave her a frowning look and said, "No. You want sugar in your coffee? There's milk but no cream."

He was drinking his black, so she said, "I like it black." She didn't really, but she drank it, trying not to make a face.

"Did you ever know Felicia Shaw?" She was surprised to hear herself saying it.

"No," he said. "Heard of her. She left town a long time ago, I guess. A singer or something. Why?"

"I just wondered. She was in my father's class in school."

"Oh."

"How old is your sister?"

He gulped down the rest of his coffee and jumped up. "Look, I have to run. I'm due at work over to the motel. You stay here till the rain lets up, okay?" He pulled the fire screen into place.

"Do you work at the motel?"

"One of my jobs. Handyman." He rummaged in the hall closet for a blue waterproof anorak with a hood. The blue, Tracy noticed, was the same color as his eyes and Miss Story's, vivid blue.

Thunder rumbled, sounding farther off, but it was still raining hard.

"Stick around till it lets up," he said again. "If you want to go to Aunt Es's tomorrow, meet me at the marina at nine o'clock. Be on time, 'cause I have a job there too and I can't fool around."

"All right. Thanks for the coffee and everything."

He nodded. "See ya." He went out, letting in a gust of wind and rain.

She watched him run down the street, thinking she liked him but wishing he wouldn't treat her like a little kid. He must be about seventeen or eighteen, though, and when boys get to that age, they think anybody younger is a baby. She bet he wouldn't ask Alison if she was old enough to drink coffee.

She wished he had said how old his sister was.

In front of one of the chairs there was a frame with a partly finished quilt on it. His mother must make quilts, and Miss Story made afghans. Maybe she had a shop somewhere. David certainly wasn't much for answering questions.

In a few minutes the rain began to let up. Tracy put on Miss Story's raincoat and was about to leave when a man ran up the steps and burst into the house. She jumped back, and he stopped short in surprise.

"Whoa!" he said. "Who have we got here?"

Maybe it was David's father. "I'm . . . David let me stay here till it stopped raining so hard."

"Where's Dave?"

"He just left for the motel."

The man took off his raincoat and hung it up. He

was a small man, partly bald, and he walked with a bit of a limp. But the thing she noticed most was his eyes, pale gray, so pale there was hardly any color in them at all.

"Are you David's dad?"

He gave her a strange look. "Five fathoms deep Dave's father lies. You ever read Shakespeare?"

"Some," she said, "but what do you mean?"

"Drowned. His father, his mother, his sister. I suppose he didn't tell you. He don't like to talk about it."

She was so shocked that she couldn't speak for a minute.

"You must be new around here if you didn't know that. Happened two years ago. They were out in that sailboat of theirs, and a thunderstorm swamped 'em."

"That's terrible!"

"Yeah. You want a cup of coffee?" He shivered. "My feet are soaked." He suddenly sounded like a complaining child.

"Thank you, I had coffee. Are you . . . ?" She didn't know how to say, Just who are you? without sounding rude.

"I'm Dave's uncle. Henry Polk. They call me Henny, like in Henny Penny. There's been five other Henry Polks in our family. Who are you?" He frowned. "You put me in mind of somebody I used to know." He stepped toward her, and she moved toward the door.

"My name is Tracy Stewart. We're new in town."
He stared at her. "I was just going." She opened the
door. He made her nervous, those strange eyes.

But he didn't come closer. Just turned away without saying any more and limped up the stairs. She let
herself out quickly and ran for home.

Chapter 7

❖ ❖ ❖

When she reached her own street, the rain had almost stopped. The twins came toward her on their bikes, Arnold doing wheelies to impress her.

"Where you been? Mom thought you'd drowned. Where are your shoes?"

"They're on the back steps of a house on an island."

"You're making it up."

"Cross my heart." Thinking still about David's family drowned, she felt like holding the twins close and telling them to be careful.

Arnold was telling her about the ship museum their father had taken them to and about the boat they had bought at the marina. "It's secondhand and it has to be painted, but it's really cool, Trace."

Richard was telling her about the Agawam chief who sold the town for a hundred dollars. "One hundred bucks, Sis! A whole town!"

Their mother was in the kitchen cutting up eggplant. She looked relieved to see Tracy, and when Tracy told her about Miss Story, she said, "Your father was very fond of her. We must have her to dinner."

Tracy went upstairs to take a hot shower and change into dry clothes. When she took off the sweatshirt that must have belonged to David's dead sister, it made her want to cry. She had been envying him, having his own family, and he didn't have them at all, only that weird uncle with the crazy eyes.

It was upsetting, things not being the way they seemed. Compared with David, she was lucky. Even if her family wasn't her real family, they were here. She would tell the boys and Alison about the adoption, though. People ought to know the truth about things. But what if they didn't love her so much after they knew?

At dinner her father wanted to know all about Miss Story. "Best teacher I ever had."

She wanted to ask him if he had known David's parents, but it made her feel so sad to think about them that she couldn't bring herself to ask. Instead she told them about the picture of their father in the yearbook and what it had said about him.

"Jumping Jackie Stewart!" Arnold said. "Dad, you never told us. Hey, tomorrow we get a basketball and put up a hoop, okay?"

When they had finished dessert, Tracy put down her fork and said as calmly as she could, "I bet you guys didn't know I'm not related to you."

She heard her mother catch her breath, and her father said, "Tracy . . ."

"It's a riddle," Arnold said. "What's the trick answer?"

"The trick answer is I was adopted. I'm not your sister."

"Come off it," Alison said.

"Ask Mom and Dad if you don't believe me." She folded her napkin and stood up. "Excuse me, please." On her way upstairs she could feel the silence behind her.

Chapter 8

❖　❖　❖

It seemed forever before she heard their footsteps. Alison knocked and came into Tracy's room without waiting for an answer. The twins were right behind her.

Tracy sat up. "Don't you guys ever wait till somebody says 'Come in'?"

"Sometimes we do, sometimes we don't." Alison sat at the foot of the bed, and the boys leaned against the door, looking solemn.

"We want to know what's going on," Alison said.

"I told you. I'm adopted."

"We can't get anything out of the parents. They said you'd tell us, quote, in your own way, unquote. If you're adopted, why didn't we know it?"

"I didn't know it myself till the other day."

"This is weird," Richard said. "This family is acting very irrational."

As briefly as she could, Tracy told them about Felicia Shaw and the arrangement with their parents.

Alison banged her fist on the bed. "That's cruel. Arrangement or no arrangement, we should all have been told years ago. It was awful to make you wait till that old bag died. . . . I'm sorry, I don't mean to insult your real mother."

"Insult her all you want to. I don't like her any better than you do."

"I'm confused," Arnold said. "You're still our sister, aren't you?"

"Legally, I guess."

"Listen," Alison said, "aside from having popped out of some other woman, what's the big deal? You've been our sister all our lives." She stopped a moment. "That's why I don't remember Mom being pregnant. I knew I wouldn't have forgotten that. But I remember how little you were, and at first I got mad because you got all the attention, but then I liked you a lot. Mom let me hold you sometimes." Her eyes filled with tears. "You're my sister, and if anybody tries to say different, I'll break their arm."

"Me too," Arnold said. "Both arms."

"It's only a technicality," Richard said. "It's not real."

Arnold threw himself on the bed and wrapped his arms around Tracy. "We love you. Don't ever go away."

Tracy laid her cheek on the top of his head. "I'm not going anywhere, Arnie."

"He means don't go away in your head," Richard said. "Don't think we don't belong to you."

"It doesn't make one bit of difference to anybody but Tracy," Alison said, "and you've got to see it's bound to be a shock to her. Trace, do you want to know more about this Shaw woman? I could investigate, quietly."

"Not now," Tracy said. "But thanks."

"Okay, but anything we can do, let us know."

"The Stewart Private Eyes are at your service," Arnold said.

"Tracy's tired. Let's go and give her a rest," Alison said. She gave Tracy a quick kiss on the cheek. "Hang in there, Sis. One for all and all for one."

After they had gone, Tracy felt better. They were terrific. How lucky could you get? After a while she would tell Alison about David, and maybe they could kind of get him involved with the family, make him feel that they cared about him so he wouldn't be so lonely.

A couple of hours later Alison knocked and waited for Tracy's answer. "Hey, do you mind if I sleep up here tonight?"

"Of course not." It had been a long time since the two of them had climbed into bed together to talk and giggle till they fell asleep. Tracy had missed it.

For a few minutes they talked about easy things, what they thought of the house, what their schools would be like.

"I thought maybe you knew about the adoption," Tracy said. "You've seemed kind of far away lately."

Alison didn't answer at once. "I didn't have a clue.

If I seemed different, I guess it's because I'm trying to cope with being a young adult. It's unreal, you know? Kids talk about different things, like boys and making out with guys, and smoking pot and all. Somebody's always bugging you to go for it, but I'm not into all that. It's hard to say no all the time and not get dropped because you're weird." She sighed. "You'll find out."

"I suppose so, but I don't think I care as much as you do about being part of a gang."

"I worry about not being liked."

"Everybody likes you."

"Oh, no, they don't. And I'm really scared about going to a school full of strangers."

Tracy reached for Alison's hand. "Don't worry. You'll do great."

Alison was quiet so long that Tracy thought she had gone to sleep.

Then Alison said, "Remember the horror stories we used to tell each other in bed?"

"You told the scariest ones."

In a few minutes Tracy felt Alison's hand relax, and she heard her regular breathing. Tomorrow, she thought, I'll tell her about David, and we'll figure out what we can do about him.

Chapter 9

❖   ❖   ❖

When Tracy awoke in the morning, Alison was gone. Tracy sat up quickly, looking at the clock. She was going to be late for meeting David. She should have set her alarm.

She dressed as fast as she could, telling her mother on the run that she had to meet David for a ride to Miss Story's island.

"But your breakfast . . . ," her mother said.

"Miss Story will feed me."

She ran all the way to the marina, but as soon as she walked out onto the dock, she knew she was too late. A boy was carefully painting an overturned boat, but there was no sign of David.

"Have you seen David Haskell?" she asked the boy.

He looked up, tossing his hair out of his eyes. "Yeah. He left ten minutes ago. Said to tell you if you showed up he was sorry, couldn't wait."

She was disappointed. She'd been looking forward to seeing Miss Story again, maybe asking her some more questions about Felicia Shaw. She sighed and looked down at the boat.

"Is that our boat by any chance? Stewart?"

"Yup. It's the Stewarts'. Nice boat. Won't be able to use it for a few days, though."

"Well, thanks for the message."

"No sweat."

Disconsolately she walked back to the causeway. She could go home and eat breakfast, do some more unpacking, help her mother, but she didn't feel like it.

When she came to the phone booth, she thought of calling Miss Story to explain why she hadn't come, but she didn't have a quarter. She leaned against the booth, disgusted with herself. She'd wanted to find out more about David, if Miss Story would tell her; about his family's accident, and that strange uncle.

"Yo!"

Without turning, she knew it was Rosie. Rosie was turning out to be one of the facts of life; you could count on her showing up, whether you wanted her to or not.

"Hi."

"We've got to stop meeting this way." Rosie grinned. "That's what they say in the movies." She was wheeling an old five-speed bike, its basket full to overflowing with grocery bags. "Shopping day. What you up to?"

"I was going over to see Miss Story, but I was too late to catch David."

"A lot of folks have been too late to catch David. You got to use ESP."

"You sound like my mother."

"I got to get together with her one of these days. Us sensitives have to hang together. She'll be interested in some of my incarnations. You want to hear one of my best?"

"Not terribly," Tracy said. "I don't believe in that stuff."

"This one'll knock you out. I was a silent movie star, see, the tragic kind, big star. My name was a household word. But my lover ODed because I wouldn't elope with him, and it was front page in the *National Enquirer*."

"I didn't know they had the *Enquirer* back then."

"Whatever. So I had to flee the country, you know? With just the clothes on my back and half a million in negotiable bonds. Guess where I went?"

Tracy sighed.

"Arabia! You heard that old song, 'I'm the sheik of Araby, into your tent I creep'? That was the kinda life I was leading in the desert sands of Arabia. I mean, it was *exotic*. Veils at all times."

"You're goofy," Tracy said.

"No, you're just not onto the wavelengths. Your mother would understand. What sign are you, Tracy?"

"Cancer."

"Figures. You're the suspicious type. Well, see you around."

"I'm sure," Tracy said.

"I got laid off for a week. Spilled a bowl of chowder in a guy's lap. Some tourist. He was very unreasonable about it. Maybe I'll drop by and see your mom later. Oh, that reminds me, my mother wants to see your father."

"Why?"

"They were in school together. Tell him Big Bertha wants to see him. Same house she always lived in. He'll know. She wants to see you too, but separately."

"Separately?"

"By yourself. I'll tell you when she's ready. She said tell your father sorry she can't visit him, but she's got this bad arthritis, rheumatoid. Can't get around."

"Oh, I'm sorry. Are you an only child, Rosie?"

"*Dusty* Rose, please. No, I have a brother off in the army. He sends a postcard once in six months. Who needs him? Well, see ya." She pushed the overloaded bike up the street.

Tracy watched her go. Why should Rosie's mother want to see her? Big Bertha? She realized she didn't know Rosie's last name. Did she have a father? It would be nice to find a whole, complete family with no parts missing. She'd always taken families for granted. Although now that she thought about it, a couple of her friends at school had divorced parents, and her best friend Susie's father was dead of lung cancer. She had never stopped to notice how mixed up people's lives were.

She decided she was hungry. Her mother was sitting at the kitchen table, studying a typed sheet of paper.

"Missed my boat," Tracy said. She buttered a couple of her mother's freshly baked cranberry muffins and poured a glass of milk.

"Tracy, this is very interesting." Her mother shoved her reading glasses up onto her forehead. "I called Bertie and asked her to work out your reading. Wait till you hear how it's right on the button."

Tracy groaned. How much spirit world was she going to have to take in one day? Bertie was an astrologer and one of her mother's dearest friends. Bertie was short for Albertina.

"What's Bertie got to say?" She didn't really care, but her mother would be hurt if she didn't listen.

"She says your sign is in the . . ." She broke off, seeing Tracy's expression. "I'll skip all that. What it amounts to is, you are going through a troubling and sad time. Now, mind you, she knows nothing about your adoption. She says"—Tracy's mother pulled her glasses down—"life will be very confusing for some time. People near to you are suffering from a great tragedy. Oh, dear, I hope it's not us."

"No," Tracy said, "I know who it is."

"But things will look brighter by the time of the harvest moon."

"Well, that's nice," Tracy said. "I'm going for a bike ride, Mom. Can I get you anything?"

"Would you stop at the drugstore and get me a tin of those Curiously Strong Peppermints? You know the kind I mean, in the square tin? English?"

"I know." She put her mother's five-dollar bill in her pocket. "I'm going to call Miss Story to tell her why I didn't come."

But her mother was already absorbed in the horoscopes again.

Miss Story sounded better. "Sorry you missed Davey," she said, "but he works on a tight schedule, holding down three jobs the way he is. Maybe you can catch him tomorrow. I'd love to see you. And, yes, I feel better. Hobbling around on my two canes, doing fine."

"I'll be sure to make it tomorrow. I have a lot of things to ask you."

"Fine. Do you like indian pudding?"

"I never had any."

"Tomorrow you'll have some."

When she had hung up, Tracy got her bike from the garage and decided to just cruise around town, see what it was like.

There were not many stores along the main street. After she passed the motel, she came to a small grocery store, a place that sold ship's supplies, and then the drugstore. Better get the mints before she forgot.

The druggist was a tall thin man who seemed glad

to have someone to talk to. He had to scrounge around for the mints. "Not many folks call for these. They're real good, though. You new in town? Summer folks?"

"No. We just moved here. My father is Jack Stewart." She wished she had a sign to hang around her neck so she wouldn't have to keep telling people that.

"Say, I remember Jackie Stewart. Wizard basketball player. He was a few years younger than me. Nice fella. You tell him Rick Fuller said hello."

She turned up a side road near the drugstore, a winding street with houses spaced far apart. A few people were working in their gardens, one man was mowing his lawn. Almost all of them waved or called out "Good morning."

She came to an open area of fields with a hill in the background. On one side of the road two horses were grazing. Then around a bend in the road there was old cemetery. An unsteady-looking iron arch supported on metal posts was twisted in a flower design. After leaning her bike against the fence, she walked in. Just inside the gate a tall stone monument listed the names of men who had died in the Civil War.

Tracy read the names, looking for a Shaw, but there wasn't one. No Stewarts either.

She wandered along through the graves, reading the names. Some of them dated back to the seventeenth century. In the oldest section many grave markers had fallen over and split. She had to get down on her knees to see the names.

She walked toward the far side of the graveyard,

where a wooded hill rose. Here and there in the cemetery itself tall trees cast shadows on the gravestones.

She was almost to the wooded end before she found what she was looking for: A plain granite headstone that read SHAW at the top. The names and dates below it were: DANIEL, 1919–1969; AMELIA, 1921–1972; BABY GEORGE, 1948–1949.

As she studied it, she heard a car on the road, heard it come along and stop. Used to city caution, she wondered for a moment if anyone would steal her bike. But then she forgot about it.

She wondered if these were her Shaws. There didn't seem to be any others. If they were Felicia's family, Felicia herself must have been buried in New Mexico. If Daniel and Amelia were Tracy's grandparents, they had died while Felicia was still in her twenties. Poor little Baby George, one year old, would be Tracy's uncle. She knelt in front of the stone, tracing the names with her finger. It made her feel connected to them.

The Stewarts were not a close family; her dad's parents were dead, and both his brothers lived in California. She vaguely remembered her North Carolina grandparents, who of course were not really related to her at all. When Tracy was four or five, the family had gone down there for Christmas. The twins were babies then, and she remembered it as a fairly confused vacation. Now those grandparents were dead.

She tried to imagine what these Shaws had been like. Maybe Miss Story could tell her. Daniel. Amelia.

Old-fashioned names, but she liked the sound of them. If George had lived and she had known him, she'd have thought up a nickname for him. He must have been a year or two younger than Felicia. She wondered if Felicia had liked him or not. Felicia sounded like a person who would want all the attention herself.

Maybe at the town hall she could find out where the Shaws had lived. If the house was still there, she could go and look at it. It was hard putting together your past out of information on gravestones and in town records. Anyway, all these Shaws would have been dead before she was born, so she wouldn't have to think about whether they had approved of her birth or not.

She got up and walked slowly back on a different path, to make sure she hadn't missed any other Shaws. If there weren't any, Daniel and Amelia must have moved here from somewhere else. Maybe even another country. Shaw sounded English. It would be fun to be English. Of course she would never know what her real father had been—besides being a person who ran out on his responsibilities.

She saw several plots with STORY on the headstone, and lots of BURNHAMs and HASKELLs. David's family were probably buried in the newer part of the cemetery, toward the fence. She thought of looking for their graves, but suddenly it all seemed too sad. It seemed okay to look at the headstones of people who had been dead twenty or twenty-five years, but the deaths in David's family were too recent and tragic.

As she turned toward the entrance to leave, she

heard a sound behind her. Before she could turn, someone grabbed her roughly by the shoulder. She thought she was going to faint. It was only in Halloween stories that skeletons rose up from their graves and grabbed you.

Her heart was slamming against her ribs as she was jerked almost off her feet.

"What you following me for?" It was David's uncle, Henry Polk, and he looked very angry.

She got her voice under control. "I'm not following you. Are you crazy or what?"

He shook her hard. "Don't you say things like that to me." He looked completely different from the rather smooth, sly person she had seen at David's house. What was the matter with him?

"I got here before you did. There was nobody here. Anyway, what would I follow you for?"

"I know what you're up to. Davey put you up to it. I won't stand for it, you hear me?"

She saw that he had a bunch of wildflowers in his hand, and she remembered that David's mother was this man's sister. Maybe he went crazy with grief when he came here. Whatever it was, she had to get out of there. The man looked insane.

With a sudden hard jerk she freed herself from his hands and ran. He yelled, but she didn't look back to see if he was following. The car he must have come in, an old blue Chevy with one front fender painted black, stood just outside the gate.

She grabbed her bike and rode past the car toward town as fast as she could go.

Just as she thought she was safe, she heard a car coming along behind her. She stood up and pumped the pedals with all her strength. A couple more minutes and she would be in the area where there were houses. He wouldn't dare touch her there.

The car behind her came closer, slowed. The driver blew the horn. She was going so fast, and she was so scared, she hardly noticed the road. Her bike hit a pothole, veered off into some bushes, and pitched her off.

"Hey, I'm sorry! Did I scare you?" The driver was coming toward her, and it wasn't Henry Polk at all. It was that friend of her dad's, Horace somebody. He was helping her up. "Darned fool thing for me to do, blowing my horn right behind you. Are you okay?"

Shaking, she let him help her up. "I'm all right. I hit a hole in the road."

"You were goin' like a bat outta hell. Here, let's put your bike in the back of the wagon, and I'll drive you home."

She felt too weak to protest. And it felt wonderful to sink into the front seat of the station wagon. "You don't *have* to take me home," she said, but she wasn't going to argue.

"No trouble at all. Anyhow, I owe you fellas one; your mom and dad invited me to dinner tonight. I'm lookin' forward to it, I can tell you. An old bach like me gets sick of his own cookin', although I'm here to tell you, I can put together a mighty fine clambake, and we'll have to do that a little later on." He glanced at her. "How come you were racing down that road like all the demons were after you? Something scare you?"

She hesitated. "I was in the cemetery looking at some of those old gravestones." For a moment she longed to tell him who her mother was. He had been in love with Felicia once. "Somebody grabbed me, and I didn't know anybody was around, so it scared me." She tried to laugh. "Pretty dumb. I guess I thought it was a ghost."

Horace looked in the rearview mirror. "That ghost happen to be named Henry Polk?"

"Yes. I guess he didn't mean any harm. I just panicked."

Horace looked grim. "Henry's a good man to stay away from. Sometimes he's all right, and other times he just ain't right in the head. David's mother took care of him as long as she lived, babied him, y' know. He was her little brother. But if Davey had good sense, he'd get Henry to a head doc and wash his hands of him. No reason he has to ruin his life over Henry Polk. One of these days I'm going to call that lawyer in Boston, the one who's executor of the will and handles Davey's money till he's of age. He's not a family friend, he wouldn't know about Henry, but maybe he could talk Davey into listening to reason."

Henry Polk's car passed them, Henry bent over the wheel, looking neither right nor left.

Horace shook his head. "He didn't hurt you, did he?"

"No, I got away from him. I don't think I'll mention it to my parents or David. I don't want to worry them."

Horace frowned. "I'll keep mum if you'll promise me to stay out of Henry's way and let me know pronto if he bothers you."

"I promise."

He let her out at her house and got the bike from the car. "I'm looking forward to your mom's cooking." He smiled at her. "Glad I ran into you. Or I should say glad I *didn't* run into you."

"I'm awfully glad you came along. Really. Thank you."

Her mother looked up as Tracy came in. She was studying her gourmet cookbook. "Hi, honey. Where've you been?"

"Oh, around. What's for dinner?"

"Chicken kiev and Horace Webster."

"Perfect," Tracy said.

Chapter 10

❖   ❖   ❖

Tracy was fifteen minutes early at the marina the next morning. David introduced her to a tall man in white shorts and a T-shirt that read RIVER MARINA. He was blue-eyed and bald, with a beard cut close to his chin.

"This is Deland Haskell, one of my two hundred cousins. He owns this outfit, works me to death."

Deland Haskell grinned. "Got to keep him out of trouble, don't I? Glad to meet you, Tracy. I expect everybody's asking you how your dad is, but I won't ask you, 'cause I don't remember him. Heard of him, though, best basketball player the town ever had."

"Which isn't saying all that much," David said.

Deland Haskell showed Tracy the boat her father had bought. "She's almost ready to launch. Nice little boat, got a good motor in her."

"Belonged to a little old lady in boat shoes," David said.

"Matter of fact, it belonged to my daughter, and she hardly ever used it. She's a tennis freak."

Tracy heard a familiar yell from the street. The twins ran down to the dock, Arnold clutching a large cardboard box. The box cover had several holes punched in it.

"They're my brothers," Tracy said. "What's up with you guys?" They seemed more excited than usual.

"Guess what we found!" Arnold's eyes were sparkling.

"Only we can't keep it," Richard said. "Mom's allergic."

"Well, what is it?" Tracy said.

With a dramatic flourish Arnold took the top off the box. "Behold!"

A fuzzy white puppy with big dark eyes looked up at them.

"Oh, he's beautiful," Tracy said. "Whose is it?"

"It's a she, and she's ours. We found her in this box behind the town hall. Somebody just threw her away—can you believe it?" Richard said.

"I'm the one saw her first," Arnold said.

David was frowning thoughtfully at the pup. He put his finger under her chin. "Where'd you come from, girl?"

"You know who she reminds me of?" Deland Haskell said.

"Yeah. In a way," David said.

"We can't keep her, though, can we?" Richard looked at Tracy as if hoping she would contradict him.

She shook her head. "No. Mom would have a

sneezing attack first thing." To David she said, "Our mother is allergic to cats and dogs."

"Blast!" Arnold said. "All we can ever have is tropical fish, and I am *sick* of guppies. They never even look at you."

"How about it, Dave?" Deland Haskell said.

David lifted the pup out of her box and held her up, close to his face. "About six or seven months old. Maybe eight. She needs some fattening up."

The pup craned her head forward and gave David's cheek a swipe with her tongue.

"She likes you," Richard said.

"Well, we could try it out." To the dog he said, "You'll have to like boats, or it won't work." He held her against his chest.

He must have had a dog, Tracy thought, one that looked something like this one. Maybe it drowned with his family? David had an expression she couldn't quite figure out, like part sadness, part as if he'd found something he'd lost. His cousin was watching him.

"Will you take five dollars for her?" David said to the twins.

Arnold's face lit up, but Richard said, "No, we can't take money for her. She isn't ours."

"Well, thanks. Anytime you want to come see her, you do that."

"What are you going to name her?" Arnold asked. He patted the puppy, who squirmed and wagged her feathery tail. "She must have been awful scared in that box."

"What are your names?" David asked them, but when they told him, he laughed. "I can't name her Richard-and-Arnold, I guess."

"You could name her Alison, for our other sister," Arnold said.

"Allie." David touched the pup's nose with his own. "You want to be called Allie?" He laughed. She wriggled and wagged her tail.

Personally Tracy thought that her own name would be better, but nobody had suggested it. That's how things went when you had an older sister.

"Shall we take her on a trial run?" David said to Tracy. "We'll get Aunt Es to feed her. I'll have to get some food for her when I come home. Thanks a lot, you guys."

"You're welcome." The twins raced off.

Someone up on the street was blowing his horn. They all looked up. Tracy took a step backward when she saw Henry Polk in his old car with the black fender. He was beckoning to David.

"Later," David shouted at him. "Let's go, Tracy." He handed her the dog and held the bow of his boat while she got in.

Henry was still blowing his horn in short, angry blasts as they pulled away from the dock.

"That was your uncle, right?" Tracy said.

"Yup." He maneuvered the boat into the channel. "You met him?"

"Not exactly, but he came to your house before I left, after that thunderstorm."

He looked at her sharply. "Give you any guff?"

She shook her head.

"As Aunt Es would say, he's the cross I bear. How's that pup doing?"

"Fine. She acts as if she's used to boats."

"Maybe she is." He studied the little dog. "She looks to me like part schnauzer, part poodle. I had a dog like that once. She reminds me of her." After he said that, he gave his attention to steering the boat.

Tracy wanted to ask questions, but something in his face made her think she had better not. She wondered if what Henry Polk had said about his family was true, and if the dog was with them when they drowned. She could ask Miss Story.

Miss Story was waiting on the front steps as they chugged in to her dock. She waved one of the two canes she was using.

"She's lookin' better," David said. "I'll come up for a sec, but I can't stay. I'm Deland's water taxi. Some of these fellas that keep their boats at the marina like to be brought from home by boat, instead of driving over. I guess it makes 'em feel like old salts." He tied the lines and followed Tracy up the path. "Look what we got, Aunt Es. New member of the family."

For a moment Tracy glowed, thinking he meant her, but then as he took the puppy and held her out to his aunt, she realized that he meant the dog. She felt like saying, Enjoy, puppy. Families are where you find them.

David was telling his aunt about the twins finding

the puppy. Tracy had never seen him so animated. The dog was good for him.

"Housebroken, do you think?" Miss Story asked.

"Let us pray," David said.

"She must be hungry. Why don't you give her some of that good steak we didn't finish last night? Puppy, are you hungry?"

The puppy cocked her head to one side and looked at Miss Story, her floppy ears moving forward.

"There's your answer," David said. "I'll feed her and take her for a very short walk." He looked at his watch. "His nibs, Mr. Ronald Davies, expects his boat-chauffeur to be on time."

When he and the dog had gone out the back door, Miss Story said, "David spent last night here, and I hope tonight. He cooked me a scrumptious steak."

They heard the dog bark.

Miss Story laughed. "The gulls are probably trying to steal her steak. I feed them, which everybody says is crazy. I agree, but I keep on doing it. They're not nice creatures, sea gulls, but they look so beautiful soaring through the sky."

The dog barked sharply again, and they heard David laugh.

"I expect she reminds him of Wendy. Same type of dog."

"What happened to Wendy?"

"She drowned." Miss Story looked away for a minute. "They all drowned, you know, his mother and dad and his sister."

"That's so awful, I can hardly imagine it."

"Don, David's father, was an expert sailor. He'd had a sailboat all his life. But they got caught in one of those freak waves that come out of nowhere. Nobody could reach them in time."

"Henry Polk said it was a thunderstorm."

"It was the tag end of a storm. . . ." She looked at Tracy sharply. "You've run into Henry, have you?"

She told her briefly about seeing him at the house and later at the cemetery. "He's kind of scary."

"What happened exactly?" She listened closely as Tracy told her. "He may feel hostile toward you because he found you in the house. Henry's mind has never worked straight. The only person he ever cared about was David's mother."

"You mean he might think I was trying to move in on her space or something? Just because I was in the house?"

Miss Story looked worried. "Who knows what Henry thinks? I wish David would sell the house and get away from here. He was planning to go to Cornell in the fall. Now he talks about waiting a year. I don't like it."

"You mean he'd put off college to look after his uncle?"

"That's only part of it. I think giving up the house seems to him like losing his last connection with his family." She shook her head. "He keeps their bedrooms just the way they were. It's morbid, you know, it really is. One can't live in the past." She paused. "I think it would be a good thing to tell David about Henry bothering you."

"Oh, I hate to do that. He'll be upset."

"He needs to be upset. Henry is getting worse. David has to face it."

"Oh." Tracy could see the point, but she hated to do it.

"You don't have to make a big thing of it. Just tell him when it seems like a good time for it." She eased the cushions at her back. "Bill James came over last night and strapped my back. I have to admit it feels a lot better. If you folks ever need a doctor, Bill is good. Looks about seventeen years old, but he knows his business."

"Miss Story, can I tell you something?"

"Fire away."

"I just found out I'm adopted."

Miss Story didn't look as surprised as Tracy had expected. "That's a startling thing to find out, I expect."

"Did you know it? You don't seem surprised."

"I didn't know it, but you put me in mind of someone I knew a long time ago."

"That's what David's uncle said."

Miss Story frowned. "He did?"

"My real mother was Felicia Shaw."

Miss Story nodded. "I thought as much. I couldn't figure out how that came about, but you do favor her, especially the eyes and the shape of the face."

Tracy told her what she had been told about her

birth and the reason she had never known about it till now.

Miss Story shook her head. "How like Felicia. Mystery. She loved mystery. It's a pity she threw her life away. She had so much to offer. She used to sing here too, you know, at school things and such. All talent and not much self-discipline. But you couldn't help loving her and wanting to shake her to make her behave."

"Do you think I'll turn out like that?"

"Oh, no. You're not that kind of girl at all. I don't believe, you know, that we're so rigidly shaped by our genes. You've grown up in a stable, intelligent, loving family. I would say, by and large, Tracy, you came out a winner. But I don't like Henry noticing the resemblance. He was sweet on Felicia."

Tracy shivered.

They heard the dog barking and David whistling to her, and a minute later they came into the house.

"That's some dog!" David said. "She took on three mean old sea gulls and scared the pants off 'em."

Tracy laughed, trying to picture sea gulls in pants.

"I have to get going, or Mr. R. D. will be pacing the dock. Be back after a while." He picked up the dog. "I think I'll take her along. She might as well get her sea legs."

Tracy stood in the doorway watching David and his dog run down to the dock. She could hear him whistling as he put the dog in the boat and untied the lines.

"I haven't heard Davey whistle in a long time," Miss Story said. "It sounds mighty good. Bless you for that dog."

"Not me," Tracy said, "it was my brothers. But I'm glad too. David's face looks different, not so closed up."

Later when they had had lunch and were playing a game of Scrabble on the kitchen table, Tracy asked Miss Story where the Shaws had lived, and if those names on the gravestone were Felicia's family.

"Yes, Dan and Amelia. Nice, quiet folks. They never knew what to make of Felicia. And they did spoil her, partly on account of the little boy having died. He was only a year old. He was born with a heart defect. Dan was a carpenter, worked in one of the shipyards."

"Did Felicia leave here right after high school?"

"And never came back, as far as I know. Broke poor Horace Webster's heart. Dan died three, four years after Felicia left, and Amelia a few years after him. The town was upset because Felicia didn't come home for the funerals; but she sent what the papers like to call floral tributes, huge ones, must have cost her a pretty penny. I believe she was in New York when her father died, singing in some little nightclub or other. Felicia never made the big time, but she always seemed to have a job. The only person I know of that she kept in touch with was Bertha, young Rosie's mother. They were cousins."

Tracy stopped in the middle of laying out a six-letter word on the Scrabble board. "Then Rosie and I are related!"

"Kissin' cousins, you might say." She laughed at the look on Tracy's face. "You could do worse. Rosie's got more sense than she lets on, and her heart's as big as a house. She hasn't had an easy life, with Bertha not able to get around."

Tracy finished her word on the board, CROWDS, with the W on a triple space. "That puts me four points ahead of you, Miss Story."

"I'd better look to my guns here." Miss Story studied the board. "You asked where the Shaws lived. The house is gone now. There's a gas station, catercorner from the drugstore." She used the O in Tracy's crowds to make HORDES.

Crowds and hordes, Tracy thought, all falling into my life from out of the blue. A mother, grandparents, cousins, a dead baby uncle. She needed to draw a new map of her life. And yet underneath the new one, the old one was still there: Alison, the twins, Mom and Dad. Out of all that confusion she would have to figure out just who *she* was. It would take a while.

She used the S in HORDES to make SUSHI. "If that's how you spell it," she said. "And I'm out."

Chapter 11

❖ ❖ ❖

Three days later the Stewarts' boat was launched.

"There's no reason," Tracy's father said, "why a little old outboard can't go in style, like the big ships. We'll have a party." He'd bought a big grill that he was almost as proud of as he was of the boat. "It'll do chicken, roast beef, steak, fish—you name it, we cook it." He set it up on the patio.

He had invited Miss Story and David; Horace Webster; the town clerk named Miss Dotty, who had been in school with him; two friends Alison had made—one a boy, one a girl; a boy the twins had gotten acquainted with; the druggist and his wife; Deland Haskell, who owned the marina; the neighbors; and Rosie.

Tracy's mother was to break a bottle of champagne over the bow. Her horoscope assured her the christening would go well.

Tracy had been so concerned with other things that she had paid little attention to the boat.

"You don't know what we named it, do you?" Arnold said, just before the family left the house.

Tracy shook her head. *"Sea Sprite? Jackie's Fireball?"*

Richard laughed. "I like *Jackie's Fireball.*"

"But that isn't it," Arnold said, tugging at her arm to get her attention. "We had a conference and we voted—"

"Don't tell her," Alison said. "Let her see it."

Most of the people who had been invited were already at the marina, Miss Story sitting in a deck chair with one of her canes across her knees. David's little dog was scampering everywhere, sniffing and inspecting everything. Alison and her friends perched on an overturned rowboat, exchanging jokes and managing to look a little above it all.

"Come look." Arnold dragged Tracy to the boat, where it was poised on ways, ready to slide into the river.

"Close your eyes," Richard said. He took her hand and led her close to the boat.

"Don't walk me into the water," she said.

"Now you can look!"

She opened her eyes and saw the name on the bow in bold blue letters: TRACY.

She was so surprised and touched that she couldn't think of anything to say.

"You get the message?" Richard said.

She bit her lip, afraid she would get tears in her eyes. She knew her parents were watching, and even Alison had an eye on her.

"It means you're our sister," Arnold said, leaning toward her to make sure she was listening. "It means you belong to us, get it?"

"I get it," she said softly. "I get it." She wanted very much to hug the twins, but they would hate that in front of their new friend and all those people. "I like it," she said. "I love it."

Arnold raced over to their father and mother. "She likes it!"

Miss Story was watching her too. She nodded when Tracy looked at her, nodded and smiled.

Rosie, the last one to arrive, came racing down the street in her lopsided, long-legged run. "Sorry I'm late," she yelled. "Unforeseen circumstances. Let's get the show on the road, folks."

"That Rosie," Miss Dotty said, laughing. "Don't she beat all?"

Tracy's mother put her arm around Rosie. "We wish your mother could have come."

"So does she. I got to make a complete report. And she sent a talisman, for good luck." She held it out to Tracy's father, a bottle of homemade wine. "Dandelion wine, four percent alcohol. You break it over the bow and the gods of the wind and the rain will smile upon you."

"We've already got—," Arnold began, but Tracy stepped on his bare foot, and Richard hissed something in his ear.

When they were ready to launch, the bottle of champagne had disappeared, and Tracy's mother stood at the bow with the wine bottle upraised.

Alison stepped forward to do her part, looking a little self-conscious and pleased with herself all at the same time. Raising her voice so they all could hear, she said, "Into the arms of the river we send our good ship *Tracy*."

The twins' freckle-faced friend said in a puzzled voice, "But it's just a secondhand outboard—" And then he said, "Ouch!" as Arnold jabbed him in the ribs.

Their mother brought the bottle of dandelion wine down with a smart crack on the immaculate white bow. It broke, and the crowd cheered, and just as Deland and David released the blocks that held the boat in place, David's dog leaped into the boat and traveled with it into the water. She looked back at David and gave a surprised yip.

The dog jumped out and leaped into David's arms for safety as Tracy's family got into the boat. Her father rowed it a short way upriver, then brought it back and tied it up at the dock.

"Everybody over to our house," he called. "Food! Beverages! Friendship!"

Tracy and Alison exchanged looks.

"He's really happy to be back here," Alison said.

"I know. How about you?" She glanced at Alison's new friends.

"Not bad. But tomorrow I'm going into town to splurge with my good old Boston chums. Lunch at the Parker House. A matinee. Dinner on T-Wharf. Esplanade concert. And sleeping over at Betsy's. Life in the fast lane!"

"I wonder," Tracy said later to Rosie, "if there were ever so many people in this backyard before."

"Not likely," Rosie said. "The people who lived here were old all their lives, you know? They always reminded me of Raggedy Ann and Raggedy Andy. Kind of stuffed. And no kids." She finished off a chunk of swordfish. "Your father is a real gourmet cook."

"Mom is saving some of the good stuff to send home to your mother."

"That's nice." Rosie's voice was unusually quiet. "She'll like that."

"Rosie, come in the house a sec. I want to tell you something." Tracy was acting on impulse. She had not intended to say what she was about to say.

In the front of the house the noise from the backyard was faint. Rosie was inspecting the house. "You folks have done a nice job on the old place. I thought it would smell musty and be all dark paint."

"It was," Tracy said. "Rosie, I don't know how you'll take this, but you and I are cousins."

Rosie looked only mildly surprised. "You mean

one of those deals where your dad's great-uncle so-and-so was a third cousin of my mother's great-grand-father?"

"I think it's closer than that. Your mother and my mother were first cousins. That makes us second cousins."

Now Rosie's eyes widened. "I didn't know your mother even came from here. I thought she was from the South somewhere."

"She is. But she's not my birth mother. I was adopted."

"You're kidding!"

"I didn't know it till we moved here. It's been kind of a shock."

"Then who was your mother?"

"Felicia Shaw."

Rosie threw her arms up. "For real? Felicia?"

"For real. She asked my parents to adopt me. Because of her career." She found herself wanting to defend Felicia. "She couldn't bring me up in nightclubs and stuff."

"Felicia Shaw." Rosie sat down heavily. "No wonder my mom wants to see you. I couldn't figure that one out. She thought a lot of Felicia. I think she wanted to be like her. 'Big Bertha and Fancy Felicia,' she used to say. 'What a team!' "

"Do you remember her?"

"No. She was gone from here before I was born. But my mom has a scrapbook full of clippings about her, singing here, singing there. She was even in Hollywood for a while. Probably Mother will show you the scrapbook."

"I'd love to see it. It's kind of strange, suddenly finding out you're somebody else."

Rosie studied her. "Does Horace Webster know?"

"I don't think so."

"Tell him. He really liked Felicia."

"I will," Tracy said. "But not tonight." She suddenly felt exhausted.

"You know what?" Rosie said. "I'm glad you're my cousin." She stuck out her hand and shook Tracy's hand.

"I'm glad too," Tracy said, surprised to find that she really was.

As they started to go back to the party, a car drove slowly by the front of the house. Rosie went to the window.

"Guess who's snooping," she said.

"Who is it?"

"Henry Polk, who else? Always prowling around and spying on people. Well, just so he doesn't throw a torch at the house."

Tracy was startled. "What do you mean?"

Rosie shrugged. "I don't believe in gossiping, but I can tell you I'm not the only one in town who thinks Henny Penny Polk is our firebug."

"Oh, no!"

"Nobody's got proof, but I know for a fact the chief's keeping an eye on him."

The twins burst into the room. "Come on, you guys, you're holding up the works. Mom's about to dish out the baked alaska, and every serving has a little horoscope with it, like Chinese fortune cookies."

"Horoscopes!" Rosie said. "Oh, man! I can't wait!"

Tracy lingered at the window until Henry Polk's car had turned the corner and disappeared. Poor David. No wonder he seemed to have the weight of the world on his shoulders. She would have to find some way to help him.

Chapter 12

❖   ❖   ❖

After everyone had gone and all the Stewarts had joined in for a fast cleanup, Tracy stumbled upstairs to her room, already half asleep. It had been an exciting day.

She was almost asleep when Alison knocked.

"Hey, do you mind if I sleep up here? I feel depressed."

Tracy made room for her. "Why are you depressed? Didn't you have fun?"

"Not overwhelming."

"How come? Your friends seem nice."

"Oh, they're okay, but they seem so young. Why does everybody in this town seem so young?"

"Well, some of us are."

"But I mean kids my age. The only one who doesn't seem like a babe in the woods is that blasted David Haskell, and he doesn't know I exist."

"Sure he does, but you spent all your time flirting

with that other boy—what's his name? Todd?—so what is David supposed to do, stand in line?"

"Arnold said he named his dog after me. What does that tell you? You think a girl's a dog, so you name your dog after her."

"Oh, come on. That was just a joke. One of the twins suggested it. Actually, I've never heard him call the dog anything but Missy or Girl."

"Mr. Taciturn. Mr. Miles-Away-Somewhere. Doesn't know how to smile."

"Would you smile a whole lot if your whole family had been drowned?"

Alison was silent for a minute. "Well, I know, he had a great tragedy in his life, but he could still be human."

"Alison, you're making me mad! A great tragedy in his life . . . you sound like a headline in the newspaper: LOCAL FAMILY LOST AT SEA—GREAT TRAGEDY. 'Sole survivor says he'll stay on in the family house.' He hasn't changed one thing in their rooms, Alison. His sister's teddy bear is still on her bed. Her white sweatshirt is still where she left it. There's a tape of Linda Ronstadt still on her tape player."

"How do you know?"

"Miss Story told me. And his parents' room is the same. Nothing changed, like they're coming home tomorrow. What if we all drowned? Mom and Dad, the twins, me, all gone in seconds? Would you go around smiling a lot? Plus, David is trying to keep his kooky uncle from going off the rails. His mother looked after her kid brother, so David thinks he has to. Come on, Alison, be real. Stop thinking about how *you* feel for five minutes, and try to think how David feels."

Again Alison didn't answer for several minutes. "Well, he's certainly got you on his side."

"He's got a lot of people on his side."

Tracy was almost asleep again when Alison said, "You're talking like you're the big sister and I'm the dumb kid."

"I didn't mean to," Tracy murmured sleepily. "I just wanted you to see."

"Do you care if I set the alarm for seven? Dad is going to drive me to the Farms to catch the commuter train. I'll be in Boston a couple of days. Maybe I'll grow up while I'm gone, huh?"

Tracy was too sleepy to figure out whether Alison was being sarcastic or not. She turned over and went to sleep.

Chapter 13

❖ ❖ ❖

When Tracy came down to breakfast, Alison and their father had already left for the train station.

"When he comes back," Tracy's mother said, "your dad's going to take some of the party food to Dusty Rose's mother. There was too much for Rose to carry last night. Anyway, he wants to visit with her. She was a classmate, you know."

"I know," Tracy said.

"It was lovely of her to send the wine for the boat. Dusty Rose is going to help me put together a horoscope chart for her mother."

Tracy smiled. Her mother was the only one who took Rosie seriously enough to call her Dusty Rose. "What are you guys looking at?" she asked the twins.

"Dad made out a chart for using the boat," Richard said. "This week we all get an hour of instruction in where the channel is. We practice putting on our life jackets. We learn the basics of starting and stopping the motor and steering the boat, how to leave a dock, how to approach a dock. We practice up on our rowing. According to harbormaster's rules, Arnold and I are never to take the boat out alone, positively never. You and Alison can if you pass certain tests. Anyone taking the boat out must sign up saying what time they are leaving, what time they expect to return, where they are going."

"Jeez," Arnold said, "it sounds like Scout camp."

"Running a boat is just as serious as driving a car," their mother said. "Richard, do you want more pancakes?"

"No, thanks. We want to go down and look at the boat. Just *look* at it, Mom."

"You won't touch the mooring lines."

"Of course not. And we won't even get in it. Just *look*, Mom."

"Wait up and I'll go with you," Tracy said.

They took their bikes and left them at the back of the marina. "Lock it," Richard said to his brother.

"This isn't Boston," Arnold said.

"It isn't paradise either. Lock it, Bro."

Tracy was in front of them going down the steps to the dock. Halfway down she stopped. David was down there, painting the side of a boat. "Isn't that our boat?"

The boys pushed past her.

"It sure is," Richard said. "Why does it need more paint?"

"Maybe somebody ran into it," Arnold said.

90

All three of them ran down to the dock. Deland Haskell was standing beside David, looking grim. He glanced up when the twins and Tracy jumped the last step onto the dock.

"Your father isn't going to like this," he said.

David looked up and said hi without smiling.

"What happened?" Tracy said.

David was intent on restoring the last letters of the boat's name.

"Some vicious maniac threw a can of red paint all over the side of the boat. And that fool night watchman of mine slept right through it," Deland said.

"What a rotten thing to do!" Arnold said. "I mean, that's *awful*."

"Did they do it to any other boats?" Tracy said.

"Nope. Just this one. Davey's been working on it ever since he got here. Red paint takes some covering. If I ever get my hands on who did it . . ."

Richard was leaning off the end of the dock. "It must have been hard to do it. I mean, to get at just that one boat."

"Why us?" Arnold wailed.

Tracy was thinking of Henry Polk driving slowly past the barbecue he wasn't invited to.

David finished touching up the boat's name and stood up. He looked at Tracy.

"Tell your father I'm paying for the paint job, and if it isn't right, I'll do the whole boat over."

"David," Deland said, "you don't know for sure—"

David interrupted him. "I know, all right." He picked up an empty paint can streaked on its sides with red paint. "That can came out of my garage." He looked very upset. "So you tell your father . . . ," he said to Tracy. "No, I'll tell him myself." He put the paint cans and the brushes in the boat shed. When he came out, he said to Deland, "I'll be back. I have something to do." He ran up the steps.

"Who does he think did it?" Arnold said.

Tracy didn't answer. She was thinking of something she wanted to tell David. A friend of her father's ran a center for emotionally disturbed people like Henry, a live-in place, more like a country club than an institution. It wasn't easy to get into and it was probably expensive, but if David was interested, her father could at least fix it for David to talk to Dr. Justin. The place was in Swampscott, not so very far away.

Rosie came leaping down the steps. "I figured I'd find you guys here dreaming over your boat. Your dad's at my house hashing over old times with my mother. Are you . . ." She stopped, staring at the overturned boat. "What's with the boat?" She reached out to touch it, but Tracy grabbed her hand.

"The paint's wet."

"Paint? Do you paint your boat every day or what?"

Tracy told her what had happened. Deland had gone into his office. They could see him talking on the phone.

"Maybe he's calling the cops," Richard said.

Rosie was looking at Tracy. "Are you thinking what I'm thinking?"

"I have to talk to David," Tracy said.

"We'll stand guard till the cops come," Arnold said.

"*Cops.* I love it. We've got one cop, Billy Meyers, who's got the marine supply store, and one deputy, Pete Mills, who works down to the Gloucester shipyard. Don't expect sirens." Rosie followed Tracy up the steps. "I've got early shift today. But you and me better hold a conference about all this. David is being prosecuted by that maniac uncle."

"Persecuted," Tracy said absentmindedly.

"Whatever. So let's rendezvous at your house after I get off work. Around seven?"

"Okay."

Rosie swung off toward the restaurant.

Tracy turned back and called to the twins. "You don't need to stay there. The boat'll be all right."

"Shall we tell Dad when he comes home?" Richard asked.

"I guess."

They ran up the steps behind her and unlocked their bikes.

"Where are you going?" Richard asked her.

"I want to speak to David." She rode off in the direction of David's house. As she got nearer, she began to wonder if it was okay to tell him about Dr. Justin. Maybe it was none of her business. But she liked David, and she wanted to help him. It wasn't right that his life should be all messed up because of a creep like Henry Polk. His mother wouldn't want him to spoil his life like that. Maybe she could say that to David.

But she began to lose her nerve when she reached David's street. It might be better to tell Miss Story about Dr. Justin, and let her tell David.

She slowed down, thinking. It was funny, somebody who was irresponsible, like Felicia Shaw, could mess up her life, and somebody who was too responsible, like David, could do the same thing. Her father liked to say, Moderation in all things.

As she came around the bend in the street, she braked her bike to a stop. Henry Polk's car was parked in front of the house. She couldn't talk to David if Henry was there.

She'd better just ride down to the end of the street, turn around, and go home. She could talk to him later.

As she came along the front of the house, she heard loud voices. Somebody was yelling, arguing. It sounded like Henry. What if he hurt David? Perhaps she should go to the marine supply store and tell the police chief what was going on. Am I being a busybody? she wondered. But she now knew from experience that when Henry got into a rage, he wanted to hurt people. She wished Alison were with her to help her think what to do.

David's dog was barking. Then the front door flew open and Henry kicked the dog. The puppy yelped in pain, skittered off the steps, and ran around to the back of the house.

She started to go after the dog, then stopped as David appeared in the doorway. He grabbed Henry by his collar and the seat of his pants and threw him out.

Henry screamed and flailed his arms, trying to keep his balance as he stumbled down the steps.

"And don't come back!" David yelled at him.

"I'll get you for this!" Henry ran for his car, cursing and threatening. Tracy stood on the edge of the lawn as David came off the porch calling "Missy! Here, Missy!" He saw Tracy and said, "Where'd she go?"

"Around the back, I think." She jumped back as Henry revved the motor of his old car and headed straight at her. She leaped again and felt the edge of the fender graze her leg. Knocked off balance, she fell on the grass.

Henry's car roared off down the street.

"Are you all right? Did he hit you?" David helped her up.

"I don't think so. I'll help you find Missy." She went around the back of the house calling, "Missy!" Her leg smarted, but it was nothing serious.

They couldn't find Missy anywhere.

"She may have run away," David said. "She's not used to this place yet." He looked as if he wanted to cry.

"Let's divide up," Tracy said. "You start back there at the garage and work toward the house, and I'll begin over there by the hedge. She's probably hiding."

David ran his hand through his hair. "I couldn't stand to lose that puppy."

"We'll find her." Tracy didn't feel as confident as she sounded, but all they could do was search. Any dog found thrown away like trash in a box must not expect very good treatment from human beings. She might have run as far as she could.

Calling and calling, both of them carefully covered their area, but no dog came. Tracy couldn't give up. She went back again and looked in every vegetable patch, every stalk of last year's corn; she searched the small toolshed, calling and calling.

She scanned the back porch, looked behind the swinging hammock and the two rocking chairs and behind a burlap bag half full of apples.

David had gone around to the front of the house, but it didn't seem likely that the puppy would have gone back there. She came down the three steps of the porch and noticed a small space under the steps, partly closed in by lattice. There was a break in the lattice that hadn't been mended. It didn't look big enough for a dog to squirm through, but she had to be sure.

She lay down on her stomach and peered into the darkness. It seemed as if there was a dim white patch inside, and she thrust her hand in. "Missy?" she said quietly. "Is that you?" Her hand touched fur. "Come on out, Missy. Nobody's going to hurt you. Come on, girl." She reached in as far as she could and gently tugged at the small leg. "That's a good girl. Come on."

She felt the dog moving. "That's it. Keep coming. David will give you a Milk-Bone or something good. Come on, baby."

The puppy's black nose appeared in the opening, and then her whole face, anxious dark eyes peering at Tracy.

"Good girl! That's my good Missy." Tracy sat back and let the puppy come out by herself. She gathered her up in her arms, soothing her, and went to find David.

"You found her!" David's voice was so soft that she hardly heard him, but the look on his face was enough. He took the puppy in his arms, soothing her, stroking her.

"I told her you'd give her a Milk-Bone," Tracy said.

He gave Tracy a broad smile. "Let's do it!"

They went into the kitchen. A coffee mug with a little coffee left in it sat on the table. "Henry's." David picked it up and dropped it into the garbage can. He got Missy two Milk-Bones and a piece of chicken. "Missy, I thought you were a done dog. If it hadn't been for Tracy . . ." He looked at Tracy and said, "Hey! Your leg is bleeding. That fool did hit you."

Tracy looked down. A thin trickle of blood ran down her leg onto her sock. "I didn't notice. It's just grazed."

"Come upstairs and let me put some stuff on it. That rusty old junk heap he drives could give a person blood poisoning." He led the way up the stairs and down the hall to the bathroom, where he found a bottle of antiseptic and a box of Band-Aids. He got a wash-cloth from the linen closet, ran it under the cold water faucet, and gave it to her. "You mop off the blood, and then we can see where you got cut."

The gash was just above her knee. It smarted when the wet cloth touched it.

David looked at it closely. "I don't think it goes very deep. This will sting for a minute, though, when I spray it on."

She bit her lip while he sprayed the gash. Then he pulled the strips off a large Band-Aid and covered the cut gently. "You watch it, and if it gives you any trouble, see Doc James right away. Like if it gets red or swollen or anything. Tell him to send the bill to me." He straightened up, looking at her anxiously. "I'm real sorry that happened."

"Oh, I've had lots worse cuts than that," Tracy said. His taking it so seriously made her feel embar-rassed. "You'd be a good doctor."

He made a rueful face. "That's what I was going to do, but everything's changed now. I don't know what I'll do exactly. I have to think about it awhile."

On their way back to the stairs, he opened the door of one of the bedrooms. "That was my sister's room," he said.

Tracy stood in the doorway of an attractive room that had obviously belonged to a young girl. The light blue wallpaper had tiny silver sailboats as its design, much of it covered with posters of Paul Simon, the

Indigo Girls, Matthew Broderick, Tracy Chapman, and prints of sailboats.

A big pink teddy bear wearing a yachting cap sprawled on the blue down comforter on the bed. A white sweatshirt with the logo of the University of Alaska lay at the foot of the bed.

"I haven't given you back the sweatshirt you lent me the other day," Tracy said.

"Keep it."

She felt deeply moved that he would show her his sister's room. She wished she could think of the right things to say. Finally she said, "What was her name?"

"Chris. She'd be about your age." He paused. "I guess Aunt Es told you about the accident."

"Yes." She looked at him. "I don't know how you stand it."

He gave a pained little laugh. "Nobody gave me a choice. Well, let's go downstairs and have a Coke or something." He started to close the door and then stopped. "Are you too old for teddy bears?"

"I guess I won't ever be too old."

He went into the room and got the pink bear. "Here. One of his ears is almost chewed off. That was our dog, Wendy. She liked to chew things." He looked down at Missy, who was sitting at his feet looking expectant. "You wouldn't do things like that, would you, Missy?" He picked her up and they went downstairs.

When they were sitting at the kitchen table drinking Cokes, David said, "Aunt Es thinks highly of you."

Tracy blushed with pleasure. "I like her a lot."

"Does that cut on your leg hurt much?"

"It just smarts a little."

"I'm sorry you got into that. That was a nasty scene." He sighed. "I've thrown him out before, but this time I mean it. I can't have him abusing my dog."

"I think he's dangerous, David."

"What makes you think so?" He tipped his chair back.

"Well, people think he set those fires. . . ."

David frowned. "It's easy to blame Henry for everything. I don't know whether he did it or not. I've tried to keep track of him, but I'm not always around."

She hesitated and then made up her mind. "Maybe I shouldn't tell you this, but the other day he threatened me. It was scary."

The front legs of his chair hit the floor with a thud. "When?"

She told him about the scene in the cemetery.

David sat very still, his mouth in a tight line.

"He was coming after me in his car, but Horace Webster happened to come along and pick me up."

He was silent for so long that she began to worry. Finally he said, "And now there's the paint job on your boat." He took a deep breath. "And if you hadn't jumped, he would have hit you with his car just now." He finished his Coke and set the bottle down hard. "So it looks like time I stopped making excuses for him. Will you come with me and tell Billy Meyers what you just told me? He's our police chief."

"All right," she said.

David dialed the phone on the wall. "Billy? Dave Haskell. I'd like to talk to you for a few minutes, about Henry. You want to do it there or down to the station . . . ? Right. See you in a minute."

He hung up and said, "Let's go." He got a leash and collar from a hook in the back hall and put them on Missy. "A mite big, but it'll do."

Tracy followed him out of the house, carrying her pink teddy bear. David didn't speak on the way to the store.

Chapter 14

❖　❖　❖

Horace Webster and another man were in the marine supply store talking to Chief Meyers. They said hi to David and Tracy and left.

"Come on back to my office," Chief Meyers said. "Only two chairs, but Davey can lean against the wall." He was a tall man just starting to put on weight. His stomach bulged slightly over his belt buckle. He smiled at Tracy. "We haven't met. My name's Billy Meyers, and you're Tracy Stewart, right?"

"Yes."

"I remember your dad. Great basketball player." He sat down in a big swivel chair behind the desk that took up most of the room. "Well, Dave. What's on your mind?"

David took a deep breath. "Tracy happened to be in front of my house this morning when I was having a fight with Henry. He kicked my dog—yeah, I got a new dog—Tracy's brothers found her and gave her to me." He picked up Missy.

"Nice dog."

"Yup. Well, anyway, Henry and I were arguing, and he kicked my dog out the door. That made me real mad, so I threw him out and told him not to come back."

"Which you've done before."

"But this time I'm not changing my mind. Anyway, he was in one of his rages, and he drove his car right at Tracy here. She jumped back. . . . Good thing she has quick reflexes or he'd have run over her. As it was, she's got a nasty cut on her leg. I cleaned it up, and we were sitting around having a Coke and she told me something she thought I ought to know. You tell the chief, Tracy."

Tracy told him the cemetery story. The chief listened intently, making notes on a pad in front of him. She tried to remember everything exactly. "Mr. Webster came along and took me home."

The chief nodded. "He mentioned it."

"And now there's that paint job on the Stewarts' boat," David said. "I recognized the empty paint can. It came from my garage."

The chief looked over his notes, leaned back in his chair, and folded his arms over his stomach. "You want to bring charges against him, Tracy?"

She was startled. "I don't know." She looked at David.

"If Henry knows she charged him," David said, "he'd really go after her. Is there any other way we can do it?"

"Somebody has to bring charges before I can make a move. You know he did the paint job, but that empty can wouldn't hold up in court. Like those fires, we're pretty sure he set them, but we got no witnesses. Horace can testify to what he saw out on the cemetery road, and, Dave, you saw him aim his car at her. So we got a case, but we need Miss Tracy here to bring charges."

"Would it be all right if I ask my father?" Tracy said.

"Sure thing. Use my phone if you want." He pushed it toward her. "Do your parents know about that cemetery thing?"

"No. I didn't want to scare them." She dialed her number, and her mother answered.

"Hi, Mom, it's me. Can I speak to Dad . . . ? No, I'm okay. Tell you later." She waited for her father's voice. "Dad, could you come down to Mr. Meyers's store for a minute? It's important. . . . Yes, the boat supply place. . . . Okay, thanks." She hung up. "He'll be right down."

Chief Meyers smiled. "I like a man that don't ask forty questions before he'll do a thing."

Tracy tried not to fidget, but she felt nervous. She had put David in the position of having to report on Henry. It still seemed the right thing, but David looked awfully pale. She reached up and took Missy onto her lap.

"I wouldn't have known your dad if he hadn't of introduced himself," the chief said. "I was still in grade school when he left. But he bought stuff for that boat from me—life preservers and paint and the like of that. Mighty pleasant fellow."

"Here he is." David had been watching through the glass on the door.

The chief went out and brought Tracy's father back to the office. He looked at her. "What's up?"

"We've got a spot of trouble with David's uncle, Henry Polk, and Miss Tracy here was kind of the innocent bystander that got dragged into it." He picked up his notes and gave Tracy's father all the information.

"You should have told us," her father said to her.

"I didn't want to worry you."

"The man is slightly retarded—isn't that right, David?" the chief said.

David nodded.

"And as I understand it, he got a lot of physical abuse from his old man when he was a boy. If it hadn't been for Dave's mother, I don't know what would have become of him. Dave here has done a fine job trying to carry on the same way his mom did, and the whole town appreciates what it's cost him."

David made a sound in his throat. He took Missy into his arms and said, "Billy, you don't need me

105

for the rest of this, do you? I got to get back to work."

"Sure thing, Davey. You take off. 'Preciate your coming by."

When David had gone, the chief said, "That boy's had more to deal with than any kid his age ought to have. Now, Mr. Stewart, what we need here is somebody to bring charges against Henry so's we can get going. Your daughter's the one with the most real evidence. Dave don't like having her make the charges, because he's afraid Henry might take out after her. I see that point, but on the other hand we do need to bring Henry in before he does anything worse. What's your thinking on this?"

"Obviously the man belongs behind bars."

"He's sick in the head, Daddy. I was thinking about that friend of yours. . . ." To the chief she said, "My father has a friend who's a really good psychiatrist. He runs a place for mentally disturbed people."

"Well, that might be the answer," the chief said, "but it'd have to go through the court first. I mean, Henry Polk is not about to turn himself in to any place like that, and he can't be forced to unless the judge says so."

"Could I bring the charges on my daughter's behalf?" Tracy's father said.

"Sure you can. She's a minor. You want to do that?"

"Yes." He put his hand on Tracy's shoulder. "And we'll keep an eye on her until this man is picked up."

The chief was making out the papers. "I'll get on the horn to the boys in Gloucester. Henry used to work in the shipyard down there, unloading those container ships. A box fell on his foot and he lives on disability now, but he hangs out down there a lot."

"He limps," Tracy said.

Her father looked at her. "Trace, why don't you go wait in the car? You look white as a ghost." He smiled at her. "That's a handsome bear."

"David gave it to me. It was his sister's."

The chief looked up. "David must think a lot of you to give you anything that belonged to Chris. And don't you worry, Miss Tracy, it's going to be hard on David, us picking up Henry, but it's going to be the best thing for him in the end. You run along now, and your dad'll be with you in a minute. And thanks for all you done."

Tracy went out and got into the car. She held the bear close, and her eyes filled with tears. "Poor David," she whispered. "Poor David."

Chapter 15

❖   ❖   ❖

A week went by, and no one had seen Henry. Everyone in town knew that the chief was looking for him, and there had been rumors: Someone knew someone who had seen him in the supermarket in Ipswich; someone else had a friend who had spotted him in a bar in Beverly; but there were no firsthand reports.

David had packed Henry's few belongings and left them inside the screen door on the front porch, but for the first time ever he was keeping his doors locked.

Tracy was getting impatient at not being allowed to wander around freely, as she liked to do. The twins had appointed themselves her bodyguards. At first she was touched and amused, but it was beginning to get on her nerves never to be alone.

Tracy's father got up early every morning and worked until noon on his book, and then if the weather was good, he took the family out in the boat, teaching them where the channel was and how to operate the motor. They took turns starting and steering and approaching the dock. Arnold, always in a hurry, almost ran into the dock once or twice, but Richard became quite expert almost at once.

As soon as Alison learned all she needed to know, she went out with them less often because she had made a new friend, a girl who was a University of Massachusetts undergraduate, Patsy, and through her she met other people, both girls and boys, whom she enjoyed. Tracy envied the ease with which she made friends, but she was pleased that Alison seemed a lot happier.

Alison often came upstairs to Tracy's room when everyone had gone to bed and told Tracy about her new friends, where they had gone, what they had done. This was a change. That last year in Boston, Tracy had felt as if she and Alison were on different tracks altogether.

"I like it when you tell me all this stuff," she said.

"I think it has something to do with finding out you're my adopted sister. That sounds crazy, but maybe there's something that makes real sisters kind of compete with each other. I don't have to compete with you."

"What was there to compete with? You're the shining star in this family."

"Tracy, don't be goofy! You and Richard are the brains."

"Well, I don't think so, but, anyway, that gives me a reason to be glad I'm adopted. It's nice to have a reason or two."

"Do you feel bad about it?"

Tracy thought. "I haven't had much time to think about it lately. I've been worried about David—and myself, I guess. I kind of look back over my shoulder all the time, to make sure Henry Polk isn't there."

"My theory is he's long gone. If he can't sponge off David any longer, why would he hang around here?"

"I don't know. Henry Polk's mind works in weird ways."

"Try not to think about him. And listen, Mom wants to know how you'd like to celebrate your birthday. It's only two days away, so think. We've made and unmade a dozen plans."

The next morning when her mother asked her what she had decided, she said she would like to have a late afternoon picnic at Wingaersheek Beach. "It's down the Cape a way. Rosie says it's neat. At least start it at the beach. We can swim and hang out, and then take the food and stuff to Miss Story's. I know she wouldn't be comfortable sitting on the beach, with the way her back hurts. David gets through at the motel around four, and I want him to come. And Rosie if she can get a night off. And maybe Mr. Webster. I've never told him about being Felicia Shaw's daughter, and I think I'd like to have him know. It's kind of like a bond between us. That's all I want at the party. We'll need David's boat and ours, or Mr. Webster's, which-ever."

"What do you want in the way of food?"

Tracy considered it. The twins came in while she was thinking about it.

"Fried clams," Arnold said.

"This is Tracy's birthday," Richard said. "She gets to choose."

"Lobster rolls," Tracy said. "Potato chips, the crinkly kind. Pickles. Olives, stuffed with anchovies."

"Yuck!" Arnold said.

Alison came in, yawning. "If you're talking about food for Tracy's party, I'll make ice cream. What kind, Trace?"

"Strawberry. But we'll need dry ice. We're going to Wingaersheek Beach."

"We bought your present already," Arnold said.

"Don't tell!" Richard said.

"Who's telling?"

"Pray for good weather," Alison said. "No thunderstorms, please."

"Tracy, dear, I've worked out your horoscope, and it's very promising," her mother said. Mrs. Stewart had had her red hair cut very short, and Tracy was startled whenever she looked at her. Tracy liked it, but it made Mrs. Stewart look about Alison's age.

"Mom, you look so young, I can't take you seriously. Did my horoscope say I'm going to marry a handsome stranger and travel across water?"

Impulsively her mother put her arms around her. "I wish I were your real mom," she said softly.

"Whatever makes you think you aren't?" Tracy gave her a hard hug. "Mom is as Mom does. That's an ancient proverb that I just made up."

Alison smiled. "You know what? This sounds sappy, but the older I get, the gladder I am that you-all are my family."

"You guys are talking like a bunch of greeting cards," Arnold said. "Can I drive the boat when we go to the beach?"

"Ask your father," his mother said.

When Tracy found Rosie later in the day and invited her to the picnic, Rosie said, "I'll take sick leave. And it's no lie; I'm sick to death of that job. Yesterday I broke four dishes. They're probably getting ready to fire me anyway. The good Lord did not equip me to be a busgirl or a waitress. Sure thing I'll go to your birthday party, with rings on my fingers and bells on my toes."

David accepted too. "I can get off at four-thirty. Thursday is one of the nights I work for Mr. Anson, but he won't care if I change it."

"Who's Mr. Anson?"

"He's an old man who used to design ships. Now he makes models and sells 'em at gift shops. He's getting kind of blind, so I do the rigging and the fine work. I like doing it. You want me to take my boat?"

"Either you or Mr. Webster."

"I'll ask him. I saw Billy Meyers this morning,

112

by the way. No sign of Henry. You know, he was always talking about taking off and going to Alaska. Did I tell you that before? I never took him seriously, but maybe he's gone and done it."

"I hope so," Tracy said. "Alison says she has a feeling he's gone away somewhere."

"Alison," he said thoughtfully. "I thought she didn't like me, but lately she's friendlier."

"She thought you didn't like her."

"Oh-oh." He grinned. "We'll have to do something about that. Can't have people thinking I don't like 'em. See you later." He ran down the steps to the motel.

She groaned as she saw the twins a little way down the road. When she caught up with them, she said, "Look, I appreciate your looking after me, but you don't have to anymore, really. Nobody's seen hide nor hair of Henry Polk, and it's almost two weeks."

"He could be hiding out," Arnold said.

"I doubt it. But right now I'm going to the library, and you don't have to hang around. Henry Polk for sure is not hiding out in the public library."

Richard frowned thoughtfully. "If I were a clever criminal, I'd hide out in some place nobody would ever think of. Like the public library."

"In the stacks?" Tracy was laughing at him, but he was serious.

"No, maybe down in the basement where they keep old books."

"What would you do for food?"

"Library paste," Arnold said. "It's yummy. Okay, Sis, you're on your own, but don't blame us if you get kidnapped."

Tracy shuddered, watching the boys ride off. A joke was a joke, but the idea of being kidnapped by Henry Polk wasn't all that funny.

She went into the little library and looked through the new mysteries for her mother. A new Martha Grimes, a Robert Barnard, a Tony Hillerman; that ought to keep her happy for a few days. Then she began looking through the young-adult section for herself. She wondered what she would get for her birthday.

Chapter 16

❖ ❖ ❖

In spite of the weatherman's warning of showers, Tracy's birthday was only a little cloudy. Mr. Webster took Tracy's mother, David, Alison, and Richard in his big powerboat, and the others enjoyed a slightly unconventional ride in the Stewarts' boat with Arnold at the wheel, his father close to him to prevent any disasters.

"Arnie, you gee when you should haw," Rosie shouted above the racket of the motor.

"What?" Arnold turned to look at her, and his father grabbed the wheel.

"Look where you're going, Arnold," his father said.

Arnold yanked his new yachting cap down over his forehead and concentrated fiercely on his job. Luckily for the nerves of the passengers, there was no dock at the beach. With his father's help, Arnold stopped the boat in knee-deep water and anchored it while the passengers waded ashore carrying picnic baskets and a legless deck chair for their mother.

Counting on her knowledge of appetites, Tracy's mother had packed extra sandwiches and soft drinks to have at the beach. They swam and threw a beach ball at each other in the chilly water, and the twins, their father, Mr. Webster, David, and Alison played a fast game of ball on the sand.

"We ought to get up a basketball team, Jackie," Mr. Webster said. "Us old duffers. With Billy Meyers and Deland and Pete Mills, we could get a team together."

"Who'd dare to play against you?" Alison said. "I mean, whizz-bang fellows like you." She was sitting beside David now, and Tracy noticed that he laughed at all her jokes. It wasn't fair that Alison and David had to be almost the same age. Tracy was the one who had known David first. But if he had to fall for somebody, it might as well be someone in the family.

"I think Davey and Alison have got something going," Rosie whispered to her.

"Oh, they're just flirting," Tracy said. "Alison likes to flirt."

"Well, Davey's not a flirt. He looks serious to me."

"You're just being romantic. Hey, I'll race you to that big rock."

When she had a chance, Tracy got Horace Webster away from the others. "There's something I want to tell you," she said.

"You haven't seen Henry around?" He sounded alarmed.

"No, no, it's not that." She paused. "You may already know it, but in case you don't, my birthday seems like a good time—well, I'm adopted. Did you know that?"

"No, I didn't. Although you don't look like the others."

"Do I look like anybody you know?"

He gave her a long, serious stare. "Matter of fact, you do, but I don't see how that could be."

"My mother was Felicia Shaw."

He gave a little jerk, and it was several minutes before he answered her. "You look like her. I noticed it first thing. But I didn't see how it could be. I figured it was coincidence."

"I didn't know it myself until a few weeks ago." She told him the circumstances. "She didn't want me to know until she died."

"I figured she'd died some time ago. I lost track of her."

"No, it was just before we moved here. I'm not sure why she insisted I shouldn't be told, but I guess she didn't want some kid looking her up."

He made a sad face. "That's Felicia. I loved her, and I guess you know it or you wouldn't be telling me this; but Felicia looked out for *number one*, if you know what I mean. But, oh, Lordy, she was a beautiful woman!"

"I feel as if it makes you and me kind of like relatives."

He gave her a bright smile and put his arm around her. "Say! It does, at that! Kind of makes you my make-believe daughter. We won't forget that." He held out his big hand. "Shake on it."

She shook his hand, thinking how many people were turning out to be her family, one way or another.

"It's a nice birthday present," she said.

"You know, Henry Polk was crazy about Felicia too. He nearly drove her out of her mind, always hanging around."

Tracy shuddered. "Miss Story mentioned it."

" 'Course half the fellas in town had a crush on her—she was used to that—but Henry's such an odd-ball, you know. It was almost like he hated her as much as he loved her. She made fun of him sometimes. Felicia could be cruel."

"I wonder if that's why he goes after me. I couldn't figure that out. I mean, why attack me twice? Maybe he thinks I look like her, and so he hates me. Do you think?"

"Could be. All I know about Henry's mind is that what goes on in there would keep ten shrinks busy for years. I just hope he's gone for good."

"Me too." It made her feel weird to think that Henry might be mixing her up with Felicia.

Her father came over, holding out a beer to Horace. "What are you two conspirators up to?"

"We were just running over the American Revolution so's we could give you some help on your book," Horace said.

"You're way too late. I'm up to the Civil War."

"Oh-oh. Wrong war. Well, we'll try again some-day. When are we leaving for Es's?"

"Right about now."

Miss Story was waiting with her own contribution to the party laid out on a long table on the porch: homemade preserves; Parker House rolls; a big pink Atlantic salmon, boiled and chilled, with a sauce; and three kinds of pie.

When it came time for presents, Tracy felt like a princess, sitting on Miss Story's sofa opening one sur-prise after another. The twins' came first, with many bows and flourishes, Arnold dancing on his toes with excitement. "I picked it out," he said.

"I paid for it," Richard said.

Tracy unwrapped it carefully and exclaimed with delight at the fat blue book, with a lock, that read DIARY.

"It's for five years," Arnold said. "Just don't lose the key."

She hugged them both. "I'll write in it every day."

Miss Story gave her a beautiful afghan, one Tracy had especially admired. There was a check from Horace, a photo album from her mother, a leather-bound edi-tion of *Walden* from her father, and from Alison a white sweater Tracy had seen and longed for in a Boston shop.

David's came last. "Close your eyes. I couldn't gift wrap it. I tried, but the paper came out shredded."

She closed her eyes tight. Then she heard Alison say, "Oh, how neat!"

"No comments from the audience, please." David put something small and cool-feeling into her hands. "Okay, you can look now, and if you don't like it, tough luck. No exchanges, refunds, or credits."

She opened her eyes and gasped. She was holding a bottle about ten inches long with a perfect little schooner inside.

"David!" She looked up at him. His eyes were warm and amused, and she thought, I don't care if he does flirt with Alison; he likes me too. "Did you make it?"

"Don't be dumb, Trace," Arnold said. "How could he *make* it?"

"I made it," David said.

"It's a beautiful piece of work, David." Tracy's father picked it up and studied it.

"Well, I work with this old man who knows how to do all that stuff. He taught me."

"You could make a fortune selling those," Alison said.

He laughed. "You don't exactly knock out a dozen every day. It takes a while."

"It's the most beautiful thing I ever saw," Tracy said.

"How about coffee or a soda, everybody?" Miss Story said. "All this excitement is making me thirsty."

Rosie, who had been very quiet, managed to get Tracy out to the back porch. "I got a present for you, but it isn't much of anything. I didn't want to give it to you in front of everybody." She thrust a small package wrapped in tissue paper into Tracy's hands.

"Listen, I'd like anything you gave me." Tracy opened it. "Are you crazy? It's one of the best things of all!" It was a clear snapshot of Tracy's mother breaking the bottle of wine over the bow of the boat on the day of the launching. Tracy was just behind her, the twins were on the other side of the boat, and in the background Tracy's father, David, and Deland were grouped together. "It's fantastic! I love it."

"Well, it looks pretty chintzy without a frame, but see, I got fired off my job, like I told you, and I was broke."

"We've got frames at home. I'll find a good one. Anyway, it isn't the frame that's important. Can I show it to the others?"

"If you want." Rosie was looking pleased. "I really took it for my mother, and then I thought you might like a copy. You can put it in that picture album your mom gave you. I couldn't get Alison into focus. She kept moving around. Tell her it's nothing personal." She caught Tracy's arm. "Hold on a minute. I want to tell you something. Two things. First, my mother does want to talk to you—what about, beats me, and she won't tell me—but she hasn't been feeling good at all. Maybe next week. The other thing is, I had a dream, and I think I know where Henry Polk is."

"How could you tell from a dream?"

"Well, you aren't a true believer, but trust me.

Meet me tomorrow at ten A.M. at the dock near the restaurant. We can take my old boat, so's yours won't get scratched."

"Take it where?"

"Tell you later," she said as Alison came looking for them.

"We're waiting for you," Alison said.

When Tracy went into the kitchen, everybody began singing "Happy Birthday to You," and her mother was holding a birthday cake with candles blazing.

"Make a wish, make a wish," the twins said.

"You have to blow out all the candles," Alison told her. "Hurry up before Mom catches on fire."

Tracy took a deep breath. To herself she said, I wish they would catch Henry Polk. She blew as hard as she could. One last candle flickered, and then like the others it went out.

"This is the best birthday I ever had," she said.

Chapter 17

❖ ❖ ❖

"You're late," Rosie said when Tracy appeared at the dock.

"I couldn't help it. I had to dodge my brothers. They still think they're supposed to guard me. I feel like a prisoner."

"Well, let's get going before they see us." Rosie untied the old wide-bottomed rowboat and jumped in, rocking it from side to side. As soon as Tracy had both feet in the boat, Rosie began pulling on the oars.

"I think this is weird," Tracy said. "I don't believe in dreams. This is some kind of wild-goose chase."

"I know what I know." Rosie just missed hitting a sailboat anchored a little way from shore. "Oops. Sorry." She rowed in short, jerky strokes, the oars sometimes skittering along the top of the water and splashing Tracy.

"Slow down," Tracy said. "You're drowning me."

"Sorry about that. I like action, you know?"

"You'd better tell me about this dream or whatever."

"It was no whatever. My mother and I were talking about where Henry might be hiding out, and then I went to bed and dreamed of a place, and I am dead sure that's where he is."

"David thinks he's in Alaska."

"Alaska, my eye. He hasn't got enough git-up-and-go to make it to Alaska or anywhere else very far from here."

"Where is it you think he is?"

"About a mile from here along the river toward Ipswich there's two or three little shacks that guys used to use for overnight fishing or in the winter if they went ice fishing, although this is a salt river and it hardly ever freezes enough for ice fishing. Anyway, these shacks have been there forever. One of them had fallen down last time I was out there. I don't think anybody ever uses them anymore. They're kind of hidden in bushes and marsh grass. It would be a perfect hideout, and that is where I think Henry is."

"How could he live there? Food and everything?"

"There's a road, more like a trail, runs behind the shacks and goes clear to Ipswich. He could drive down there at night and stock up. He wouldn't be all that well known in Ipswich."

"Well, I don't see any reason to think he'd be there."

"Tracy, I dreamed of a cabin. A little shack."

Tracy sighed. "If you get tired of rowing, let me know." And I hope, she thought, it will be soon.

But Rosie kept on rowing, grazing a rock here and there, and once running aground in shallow water. Without even stopping the story she was telling Tracy about the teacher she would have in the fall, she swung one leg out of the boat, used the wrong end of the oar, and pushed off.

". . . and Mrs. Carter has asthma attacks, so every once in a while when the chalk dust gets too much for her, she takes a few days off, and you get substitutes. And of course with subs you can get away with murder. I mean, they just sit there not knowing what to do next. Sometimes I feel sorry for them."

She leaned on her oars as they came around a bend in the river. "We're getting close," she said in a low voice. "From here on, don't talk."

Tracy didn't point out that she hadn't had a chance to talk. She was beginning to feel scared. What if Rosie was right?

"Listen," she said, keeping her voice down, "we have to have a plan. What if Henry is there?"

"We go in and take him. I brought rope to tie him up." She pointed to some clothesline in the bottom of the boat.

Tracy was horrified. "Rosie! He's strong as an ox. Believe me, I know. He'd kill us. He's almost killed me once already, maybe twice. I'm not going anywhere near him."

"Then I'll go in alone."

"You will not! If you don't promise you won't, I'm getting out right here."

Rosie grinned. "And swimming back?"

"I can walk along the riverbank."

"There's quicksand here and there—I don't suppose you'd mind?"

"I mean it, Rosie. Henry Polk isn't right in his head."

"So what else is new?"

"If he's cornered, he'll be desperate."

Rosie considered the problem. "Tell you what we'll do. When we get within yelling distance, we'll stop the boat. You stay at the oars ready for a quick takeoff. I'll crawl through the marsh grass and see if I can spot him." She refused to be argued out of it, so with great reluctance Tracy agreed.

"You promise you won't let him see you? If he's there." She realized that Rosie's conviction that Henry was there had almost persuaded her that he was, but that was crazy.

Rosie rowed a little farther. "Muffled oars," she whispered. "Paul Revere stuff."

She stopped the boat under an overhanging willow tree and cautiously got out into the knee-deep water. Motioning for Tracy to take her place at the oars, Rosie went ashore, bent almost double in the tall marsh grass.

A few seconds later Tracy couldn't see her at all except for a slight motion in the grass. She held her breath, gripping the oars so tightly that her hands began to ache. If I don't think he's there—and I don't—why am I so terrified? she said to herself.

She had to admit that Rosie would be a great Indian scout. It was impossible to see or hear a thing now. And she couldn't see the shack. What made Rosie so sure it was the right place?

Tracy got out of the boat and silently turned it around. No use being headed right into enemy territory if they had to take off in a hurry.

Then it was just waiting. And waiting.

Finally, just as she had decided she had to go look for Rosie, someone just out of her sight came splashing along in the shallows. Tracy's heart banged against her ribs. If it was Rosie, she'd be silent. It had to be somebody else. Henry? She took one oar out of its lock ready to bash him.

Then Rosie came into sight, walking normally, making no effort to hide or be quiet. She slung her leg over the stern and said, "Okay, let's go, cap'n."

Tracy started rowing. She felt sick with relief.

"He wasn't there. Or the shack wasn't there."

"The shack is there, and Henry is hanging out there."

"What!" Tracy stopped the oars, staring at Rosie. "Make sense."

"He isn't there this minute, but there are tracks of his car in the back, and in the shack there's cans of beans and corned beef hash and a bottle of rye whiskey half empty, and that dirty old green nylon jacket he wears all the time. He's staying there all right."

Tracy had never rowed so hard or fast in her life.

"The first and only person we tell is Billy Meyers, agreed?"

"Agreed," Tracy said.

She looked over her shoulder at the sound of an outboard.

"It's Alison and the twins," Rosie said. "Remember, not a word!"

Alison cut the motor and drifted alongside the rowboat. "Where have you guys been? The boys were sure you'd been kidnapped. Somebody told them they saw you and Rosie going upriver in an old beat-up boat."

"It's not that beat-up," Rosie said stiffly.

"We've just been exploring," Tracy said.

"Then why do you look so peculiar? You're pale."

"I'm not pale. I'm just hot. See you back at the house, okay?"

Alison sighed and said to the twins, "You and your plots."

"We're just looking after her," Richard said.

Alison made a wide circle and headed back to town, leaving the rowboat bobbing in the wash.

Rosie, as usual, said the unexpected thing. "I wish I had a couple of brothers to look after me."

Tracy was too busy rowing to talk. As soon as they docked the boat, they ran all the way to the marine supply store.

"We have to talk to you," Rosie said to the chief.

She glanced at his young helper, who was unpacking merchandise. "Top secret classification."

Billy Meyers looked at their faces a moment and then said, "Let's amble over to the station. Tony, hold the fort for a few minutes, will you?"

They walked the block to the small police station in silence, Rosie almost teetering on her toes with excitement. Tracy had mixed feelings. She was afraid Rosie might have exaggerated what she had found. Anybody could wear an old green jacket, and a shack like that would be a good place for a homeless person to hang out. It might not have anything to do with Henry.

The chief sat down at his desk and said, "All right, what's the news?" He looked at Tracy.

"You tell him," Tracy said. "You found it."

Breathlessly Rosie told him about her dream, at which he raised his eyebrows, and about discovering the shack, the tire marks, the cans of food, and especially the jacket. "I'd know that faded old jacket anywhere."

The chief looked thoughtful. To Tracy he said, "You see all this too?"

"No. I stayed in the boat."

"For a quick getaway," Rosie said.

"Well, not only that, but I'm scared of Henry Polk. I didn't want to run into him if he was really there."

The chief nodded. "Sensible. You took a chance, Rosie."

"Oh, I could handle that smarmy creep," she said.

"Rosie, you're a very competent young lady, but don't tangle with Henry."

"What are you going to do?" Rosie said. "Are you going to take a posse right out there before he gets away?"

He laughed. "I'm a little short of posses, but here's what I'll do: I'll send Pete out there after dark to size things up. And I'll have a word with the chief in Ipswich, which would be the logical place for Henry to get his groceries."

"Just what I said," Rosie said.

He made a few notes and reached for his phone. "Thanks for the info; and now if you girls will excuse me, I'll get ahold of Pete. And do me a favor—stay away from that shack. Promise?"

They promised. Rosie left slowly, hoping to hear what the chief said to Pete, but he waited until the door closed.

"Well." She looked pleased. "We did our civic duty. Now I got to go home and get my mother's lunch. See you." And she galloped up the street.

Watching her go, Tracy thought, I don't even know where Rosie lives.

She walked home slowly, thinking about the shack. It would probably be best not to tell anyone, even the family, about what Rosie had found. At least not until Chief Meyers had a chance to check it out. She was sick of thinking about Henry Polk, about his maybe thinking she was Felicia Shaw. Actually she was sick of being Felicia Shaw's daughter. Everybody said how beautiful Felicia had been, but there was always the *but*, like "but she was an airhead, irresponsible, wild," or even, as Horace Webster had said, "cruel sometimes." And people saying Tracy looked like her. Being adopted was one thing; she could adjust to that. But being reminded of what kind of person her mother had been, that was something else. She wished they had never come back here, where everybody knew all about Felicia Shaw.

Chapter 18

❖ ❖ ❖

Rosie had gone to see the chief first thing the next morning, and she stopped at Tracy's house, called her outside, and said, "Nothing."

"Nothing what?"

"When Pete got there, there was nothing there, except the tire marks. No food, no jacket, nothing." She looked downcast.

Tracy wasn't sure whether she was glad or sorry.

"If it wasn't for the tire marks, they'd probably think I made it up."

"It could be anybody's tire marks."

"Well, that's the way the cookie crumbles. I gotta go. I got the harbormaster to let me take over Miss Story's clamming permit. I'm going digging." She had a pair of hip boots under her arm. "Wish me luck. I *hate* digging clams. See you later."

For once, the whole of Tracy's family happened to come in for lunch at the same time.

"What are you looking so pleased about, dear wife?" Tracy's father said, ruffling his wife's short hair. "Next time you get a haircut, take care they don't make you a skinhead."

"I'm looking pleased because I've found something useful to do."

"In the days I've just been reading about, providing a family with excellent corned beef sandwiches like these was fulfillment enough."

"But these ain't those days, Daddy-o," Alison said.

"What did you find to do, Mom?" Tracy asked.

"Let us guess," Arnold said. "You're going on a six-day bicycle race."

His mother laughed. "Not quite. Mrs. Keenan told me about a halfway house for teenagers in trouble. It's in Salem, and they need volunteers."

"Mom, you've got four teenagers and almost-teenagers right here," Richard said. "My main trouble is, we're out of mustard."

"No, we aren't. Look in the refrigerator."

"So what will you do at this place?" Tracy asked her.

"Whatever is needed. Mary Keenan says everything from mending their jeans to getting them interested in reading. Some of those kids are practically illiterate." She looked at her husband to see his reaction.

"If you want a serious opinion," he said, "I think it's great. I know you miss all the things you were doing in town."

"And the more kids you make literate," Richard said, "the more people there will be to read Dad's books."

"Right," his father said. "And since you-all seem to need something to do, I'm taking you to Gloucester this afternoon—assuming you want to go. There's a four-day celebration going on—Saint Peter's Fiesta. Saint Peter is the patron saint of fishermen."

"What do they do?"

"Everything. Baseball games, fireworks, parades, band concerts, and on the last day—but this isn't the last day—there's a high mass and a blessing of the fleet."

"Let's go!" Arnold said.

"Finish your lunch."

They went in the car. Their father gave them a history of the region as they drove along. Tracy and her mother smiled at each other. They had a private joke that if they could get ahold of a time machine and send him back a century or two, they would have a happy man.

When they came to Stage Fort Park in Gloucester, he told them about the Dorchester Company. "They built a fishing stage," he explained. "And in the Revolution and in the War of Eighteen Twelve it was used as a fort."

"Neat," Arnold said. "There's a cotton candy place. Can we—"

"No," his father said.

"We're really interested, Dad," Richard said. "What else happened?"

When they came to the big bronze statue of a fisherman at his helm, peering out into the waters of the harbor, even Alison was impressed. She read the inscription aloud. " 'They that go down to the sea in ships.' "

"If you want real heroes," her father said, "forget about cowboys. These guys were the real heroes."

"Why are there wreaths of flowers floating in the water?" Richard asked.

"In memory of men lost at sea."

They got back into the car and drove slowly through the heavy tourist traffic to the city parking lot. Parking places were filled, but one car happened to pull out at the right moment.

Once parked, they walked down to the pier to see the fishing boats. Crowds were everywhere. Afterward Tracy remembered mostly the noise: bands playing, ice cream vendors calling out their wares, pizza places in improvised shacks, men selling balloons, hot dog vendors, cotton candy stalls, the Ferris wheel, the merry-go-round. They had to hang on to each other to keep from getting separated in the crowd.

When everyone but the twins was exhausted, their father led them down a shortcut near the waterfront in the general direction of the parking lot. The shortcut was lined with the bars fishermen hung out in.

Alison looked up at a house on the next street that

had a widow's walk on the roof. "Imagine being a woman married to a fisherman and never knowing each time he went out if you'd ever see him again."

A group of men burst out of the bar ahead of them, laughing, some of them staggering. Tracy's father steered his family along the sidewalk past them. They had to walk single file on the narrow crowded street. Band music was getting louder.

"We'd better cross over before we get trapped by a parade," he said, starting diagonally across.

Tracy, who was last in line, looked back at the men who had come out of the bar. Suddenly she came to a dead stop, staring back at them.

"Hurry up," Alison said.

"Alison! I saw him."

"Saw who? Come on, we'll lose track of the others." Alison was already out in the street.

"Henry Polk. Coming out of that bar. He was drunk."

"Oh, it just looked like him. You've got Henry Polk on the brain. Let's go!" She dashed through an opening in the crowd.

As Tracy turned to follow her, the band music was suddenly deafening, and Tracy was caught up in a laughing, shoving mob of people marching alongside the band. People in all kinds of improvised costumes, people with their faces made up like clowns, people who seemed to Tracy like one huge creature out of a childhood fairy tale, bearing down on her, moving her along with them, laughing in her face. A man in a tattered sailor suit with a tall flowered hat grabbed her in a crushing hug, grinning with his face close to hers. He shouted something at her in Italian.

She wrenched herself free only to crash into a stout woman with two small children who yelled at her to watch where she was going.

She was in such a panic that she couldn't remember which way she wanted to go, but it made no difference; she was swept along with the crowd. All she could think of was that she would never see her family again.

And all the time the band played earsplitting music, some kind of march that went on and on.

She didn't know she was crying until some very young-looking sailor touched her face and wiped away a tear. Then he too was gone.

They passed the bar where she had seen Henry Polk. If he was still nearby, she couldn't tell; too many people.

She was afraid she would fall down and be crushed by this yelling, singing, surging mob.

All at once someone came up behind and seized her, lifted her off her feet. She thought she was going to faint.

"Tracy! Hang on to me." It was her father. "Hang on tight."

She flung her arms around him. Using one of his long arms held out stiff like a football player's, he shoved his way through the people, stepping on toes, pushing his way through, and running across the street between the tubas and the trumpets. All the time she heard him saying, "Oops, sorry, let us through, please, sorry, coming through." She heard him, but she was sure no one else could hear him.

Suddenly they were free of the crowd, going down an alley toward the parking lot. She clung to him, shaking. He stopped and put his arms around her and held her close for a minute. He seemed tall and strong, like some hero out of storybooks, and he had freed her from the monster.

"I'm so sorry, honey," he said. He pulled out a big handkerchief and wiped her tear-streaked face. "That was scary, wasn't it?"

"I didn't think I'd ever find you again."

"I'll always find you. You can count on that."

She tried to pull herself together. "I was as bad as some little kid losing her mother. I really panicked."

"Take a few deep breaths. That's it." He held her hand in his. "All right now? Everybody's back at the car, worrying about you."

Within a few minutes they were in the car park, and the twins were running toward her, then hugging her. Her mother hugged her, and Alison hugged back and kept saying she was sorry she hadn't hung on to Tracy's hand back there in that crowd.

Tracy began to realize how foolish she had been to panic so, but just the same it was nice sitting on the backseat of the Buick with her mother holding her hand and Alison close beside her.

The twins sat in front with their father. When they were out of Gloucester and on the way home,

Arnold twisted around and said, "Alison said you saw Henry Polk. Did you really?"

"Never mind that now, Arnold," his father said.

"Well, I thought I did. But there were so many people. . . ."

"We should have gone back and made a citizen's arrest," Arnold said.

Tracy began to laugh, partly out of relief at being safe with her family, partly at the picture of the twins arresting Henry Polk.

"Just in case, I'll give Billy a call," her father said, "but the festival lasts four days, and until it's over, you might as well hunt for the proverbial needle."

"In a haystack," Richard finished for him.

"Let's speak of pleasant things," his mother said.

"Shoes and sealing wax and kings," Richard answered.

"The pleasant thing I'm thinking of," Alison said, "is that Mom invited Miss Story and David Haskell to dinner next week, and if David Haskell doesn't ask me for a date by the end of the evening, I'm going to ask *him*."

"Poor David," Arnold said. "He doesn't have a chance."

Chapter 19

❖   ❖   ❖

But instead of David and Miss Story coming to dinner, on a warm July night the Stewarts joined Horace Webster and David at Miss Story's for Horace's famous clambake. Sitting on the small beach, stuffed with wonderful food, watching the moon break through the clouds and light up a path across the water, Tracy thought she had never felt happier or safer. She held sleepy Missy in her lap and wished the evening could go on forever.

David and Alison were sitting close together in quiet conversation, and Tracy smiled. Who was asking whom for a date? Alison seemed to be waging her campaign, but from the look on David's face, perhaps she didn't have to.

They had been talking about colleges. David had finally sent in his papers and check to Cornell, and he and Miss Story had been talking about having her live in his house during the winter.

"It's risky for her living here alone in bad weather," David had said to the others. "I know she's got some good neighbors on the island, but in town she can call the doc if she needs him, and get her groceries and stuff without making the trip by boat."

"And we'll have her closer to us," Tracy's mother said.

"Well, I haven't put up much of an argument," Miss Story said. "David can't just close up the house while he's away, and I have to admit it will make life easier and pleasanter for me. Although I don't know who'll feed my sea gulls."

Tracy was pleased. She enjoyed being with Miss Story. "You can help me out when I get stuck with my homework," she said.

She lay back on the sand, looking up at the stars. Nearly all the clouds had gone, and the blackness of the sky and the blackness of the water made every star more brilliant.

Horace was covering up the pit where he had cooked his clams and lobsters, the ears of corn and the potatoes. David and Alison got up to help him pick up paper plates, cups, and the rest of the debris. Tracy moved Missy off her chest and got up to help.

"We ought to be getting home," her father said. He got up, stretched, and added, "Horace, it was like old times. You always were the best clambake man in town."

"It's mighty good to have you folks here." He put his arm around Tracy for a moment. "All of you."

When Tracy was halfway up the path to the house, carrying things to be dumped in Miss Story's garbage pail, she heard the fire siren, faint at first, then louder as it wailed its lonely scream.

David and Alison were just behind her, and they all stopped. Tracy looked at David and saw him staring hard toward the mainland, trying to see the whirling red lights of the fire truck.

Tracy was in the kitchen washing off some plates when the phone rang. She started to answer it, but David got there first.

"Yeah, Deland." His face went white. "Right away." He slammed down the phone and ran toward the door.

"What is it?" Tracy said.

"My house is on fire." He raced down the dock to his boat and was gone almost before the others realized what was happening.

In minutes Horace was helping Miss Story into his boat. The Stewart family scrambled into their own, and the two boats backed away from the dock and headed for the landing at the motel. Even the twins were silent. Tracy grabbed up Missy and held her tight.

Horace was already securing the lines of his boat when the Stewarts caught up with him. "My car's in front of the motel," he said. "Pile in." He took Miss Story's arm and helped her along the brick path to the street.

"We'll run," Richard said. "We can get there just as fast."

142

Alison and Tracy ran after them as Miss Story and their parents hurried to Horace's car.

People were walking toward David's house, some of them calling out and running to help. Cars screeched around the corner, and above all the other sounds, the siren split the night with its unearthly noise.

Tracy saw Chief Meyers's car pass them, going as fast as he could through the growing crowd of people.

"It really got going," a man behind Tracy said.

Tracy gasped when she came in sight of the house. It was ablaze from top to bottom. A dozen or more volunteers were helping the firemen lay their hoses, but it was impossible to get close to the house.

Alison, right behind her, kept saying, "No, no, no, no!"

Missy was frightened and trying to jump out of Tracy's arms. She saw David before Tracy did and whimpered and struggled to go to him.

David was directing one of the hoses toward the front of the house. Someone ran up to him and put a helmet on his head, but David didn't seem to notice.

Horace Webster and Tracy's father went to help drag the heavy hoses into place. Miss Story stood close to the rope that the police had put up to keep the crowd back.

Another fire truck from a nearby town was pulling in.

Miss Story shouted to Deland as he ran past her. "Make David move back. He's too close. Dee, make him move."

Deland nodded and went to David, shouting to him to move back. David pointed to the one end of the house that was not yet in flames. Deland grabbed his arm, but David shook him off, put the hose in Deland's hands, and ran for the window. Miss Story screamed his name, and two men ran to stop him.

They caught his arms and pulled him back. Missy began to bark, and before Tracy could stop her, she wriggled out of Tracy's arms and ran toward David.

"Missy!" Tracy shouted, and the twins just behind her began to yell.

"She'll get burned," Arnold hollered in Tracy's ear.

Before Missy reached David, a stream of water from one of the hoses caught her and rolled her over, away from David. She lay still a minute.

Tracy ducked under the rope and ran toward her, avoiding the fireman who tried to stop her. Missy struggled to her feet and ran around the house to the back.

Tracy felt the intense heat of the fire as she raced after Missy, and the smoke choked her. There was a loud whoosh as part of the roof fell into the house.

For a minute she couldn't see Missy through the dense smoke, but then she saw a flash of white in the vegetable garden. Missy was running in circles, barking hysterically. There was so much noise that Tracy wasn't sure Missy could hear her, but she kept calling the dog's name as she ran toward her.

With a quick grab, she seized Missy's fluffy tail

and picked her up. Tracy heard someone was running toward her. She turned and saw that it was her father.

"I'm all right," she yelled. As she turned to circle back out of the heat and smoke, she saw a car on the next street, across the vacant lot behind David's house. The car was just driving away. It was Henry Polk's old blue car with the black fender. She pointed to it, and her father glanced at it, but he was intent on getting her away from the burning house.

"That was crazy!" he said, when they had run far enough from the house to hear each other.

"Did you see that car? It's Henry Polk's. I've got to find Chief Meyers."

"I'll find Chief Meyers. You take the dog and go sit in the car. You nearly gave us a heart attack."

She got into the car beside her mother, who was looking pale.

"What's the matter?" Tracy said. "I wasn't in any danger."

"You're a hero," Arnold said.

Richard pointed to the side of the house where Tracy had been. It was now in flames, and the grass she had been running on had caught fire.

Her father was talking to Chief Meyers. Tracy saw the chief nod and call to Pete. The two of them took off in separate cars. Tracy's father and Alison came to the car, and her father gave Alison the car keys. "Take them home, please," he said.

"Dad, tell David I have Missy. Please, it's important. He's lost everything else. Where is he?"

He pointed to one of the fire trucks. David was leaning against it, looking dazed. Miss Story and Deland were talking to him. "Don't forget to tell him about Missy."

Alison had to do some maneuvering to turn the car around. There were a lot of cars and trucks parked at odd angles, and people on foot were reluctant to move out of the way. She beeped her horn and leaned out the window. "Let us through, please. Let us out, please."

Some of them saw Tracy and the dog in the backseat and gestured their approval. They had seen her rescue Missy. She was too exhausted and upset to care, but she tried to smile.

Rosie shoved her way through the crowd and ran alongside for a few yards yelling, "Bravo! Bravo!"

Tracy leaned her head against her mother's shoulder and closed her eyes. All she could see in her mind was Chris's pretty bedroom with the silver sails in the wallpaper and on the bed the white sweatshirt that read UNIVERSITY OF ALASKA. Why Alaska? Maybe Chris had intended to go there. It was good that the pink bear had been saved.

Chapter 20

❖　❖　❖

It was more than an hour before Tracy's father came home, smoke-streaked and tired. The house had burned to the ground. David and Miss Story were staying at Deland's house, and in a day or two they would go back to Miss Story's.

The next morning Deland came by to pick up Missy.

Tracy almost hated to see the dog go, but her mother had been sneezing all morning. Missy couldn't stay. "She's calmed down a lot," Tracy told him, "but she's anxious about David."

"So are we," Alison said. "How is he?"

"Very quiet. Kind of in a state of shock. The doc came by last evening and gave him a sleeping pill. Had to argue to get him to take it." Deland accepted the offer of a cup of coffee and sat down at the kitchen table. "I can't help thinking that in the end it may all be for the best for Dave. He'll get the insurance

147

money, and all that house did was remind him of the family he lost. What does a boy going off to college need with the responsibility of a house back here?"

"Miss Story was going to live in it in the winter," Tracy said.

"We talked about that this morning. Dave and I are going to make the wing of my house into an apartment for her. My wife and my one kid that's still at home rattle around in that big house like a handful of marbles. All we use that wing for now is storage. It'll make a nice cozy apartment for her."

"Oh, that's good," Tracy's mother said. "That will give David something good and constructive to work on this summer. Have a blueberry muffin, Deland."

"Thank you, ma'am. Mighty good-looking muffins." He looked at Tracy. "Dave asked me to tell you how much he appreciates you getting ahold of his dog when she ran off like that." He stroked Missy's head. "He lost his dog Wendy in the accident, you know, and he sets great store by this one."

"We found her," Arnold said. "She'd been thrown away, just like an old box of trash. Poor Missy." He patted her, and she licked his hand, faintly wagging her tail.

Deland shook his head. "The things folks do."

"What about Henry Polk?" Tracy was almost afraid to ask.

"Should have told you first thing. Billy and Pete picked him up last night."

"Oh, good!" During the night she had dreamed that Henry Polk was throwing bombs at their house.

"Where did they find him?" she said.

"In a bar in Ipswich, drunk as a skunk."

"I thought he might go back to that shack," Tracy said. When they looked questioning, she said, "Rosie dreamed he was there. We went over the other day, and Rosie found his jacket and food. We told Chief Meyers."

"Tracy!" her father said. "You could have gotten hurt."

"Don't worry, I stayed in the boat. Rosie was the one who went into the shack."

"You never told us," Alison said.

"Chief Meyers said not to. They wanted to stake him out. Only he wasn't there when they went."

"It's interesting that Rosie dreamed that," her mother said. "She really is one of us."

"If David is looking for a lawyer for his uncle," Tracy's father said, "tell him I'd like to talk to him. I've got a friend, an old classmate, in Salem, who's good."

Deland nodded. "Dave would like to see him put into one of those hospitals for the mentally disturbed, because sure as shootin' Henry is mighty disturbed. It'll be a big load off Dave's back to have him put away."

Tracy's father walked out to the car with Deland.

"Let's get Timmy Keenan and go skateboarding," Arnold said to his brother.

"You go. I don't feel like it." Richard started upstairs.

Arnold followed him, arguing.

Tracy went up to Alison's room with her. They could hear the twins, their voices growing angry. Finally Arnold slammed the door and ran downstairs. They watched him cross the lawn to the Keenans' house.

"They don't get along as well as they used to," Tracy said. "They're so different."

In a few minutes Richard knocked on Alison's door and came in. He looked upset. "Now I'm supposed to be rolling around in a fit of guilt," he said. He flung himself into Alison's chair.

"What's wrong, Rich?"

"I'm sick of being a twin. Richard-and-Arnold, Richard-and-Arnold. When do I get to be just Richard? David's lucky, all alone in the world."

"Well, excuse us for living," Alison said.

"I don't mean you. I'm just sick of being half of a team. We even talk like a team. Remember Arnie saying he thought of your birthday present, Trace, and I said 'I paid for it,' and everybody laughed. We do that all the time, like a pair of TV comics."

"Well, just stop doing it."

"It's not so easy after all these years. Arnold wants

to go skateboarding, I want to read *Huckleberry Finn.*
He gets mad; I feel guilty."

"It's a power play, Rich," Alison said. "Acting dependent on somebody the way Arnie acts with you. Stop feeling guilty. If he gets mad, let him. In time he'll see he can't manipulate you."

Richard looked thoughtful. "Well, thanks for the psych. I'll try it." He left.

"Families," Alison said. "You can't live with 'em, you can't live without 'em."

Tracy was thinking she was glad Richard had used David as an example of someone without a family, instead of herself. That meant he really thought of her as part of the family.

The phone rang, and their mother called upstairs to Tracy. "It's for you, hon."

It was Rosie. "First of all," she said, "did you hear they picked up Henry?"

"I heard."

"Second thing, my mother would like to talk to you. She's having one of her unusual days when she feels pretty good."

"Talk to me when?"

"Right now."

"Oh. All right. I don't know where you live, though."

"I'll meet you at the end of your street in five minutes. Private escort service, low rates, try us, you'll like us." She hung up.

"Rosie's mother wants to talk to me." Tracy felt nervous.

"Whatever for?"

"I don't know. But she was a first cousin of my birth mother's."

"Oh. Maybe she's got a message from beyond." She reached out and touched Tracy's hand. "I didn't mean that. Why do I say those things? It's just that Rosie and Mom and all their otherworld stuff bring out the cynic in me." She did a double take. "Hey! That means you and Rosie are cousins!"

"That's right."

"Curiouser and curiouser." She thought about it. "Is it okay to laugh?"

"I have to go. She said five minutes. Laugh all you want to. It beats crying." She grabbed Alison's brush, looked in the mirror, and gave her hair a quick going-over. "I'm not dressed for inspection. See you later."

She ran up the street to meet Rosie, feeling more nervous every minute. What could Rosie's mother have to say to her?

Chapter 21

❖ ❖ ❖

"She won't give me a clue what she wants to talk to you about," Rosie said, "but I suppose it's Cousin Felicia. They were buddies." She looked at Tracy. "Are you curious about Felicia or not?"

"I don't know," Tracy said. "I guess it depends on what I find out."

"Well, I don't think she was a prostitute or anything."

"Good grief, Rosie!" Tracy was shocked. "I never thought she was."

"Well, she could have been. I mean, she was pretty wild when she was a kid, I know that much."

"That doesn't mean a person ends up a prostitute."

"What I said was, I was sure she *wasn't*. Relax, Trace."

Rosie stopped in front of a smallish clapboard house that needed paint. "That's where I live. I'm not allowed in on this conference, so just knock on the back door and go on in." She turned and went back down the street.

Tracy stood still for a moment, getting up her nerve. She noticed that once there had been borders of flowers along the brick walk, but they had long ago given up to the weeds. Slowly she walked to the back porch and climbed the steps. One step had a broken board. The inside door was open, and she could see into the dim kitchen. She knocked on the screen door and waited. Rosie had said knock and go in, but that seemed impolite. She knocked again.

"Come in, come in." It was a deep, impatient voice.

Tracy almost turned around and ran. Instead she took a long breath and opened the screen door.

"Don't let the flies in," the voice said.

Tracy closed the door quickly and stepped into the kitchen. After the bright sunlight it was hard to see at first. Like most older houses the kitchen was large, and it took her a moment to locate the wheelchair behind a round oak table near the window.

"Come over here and let me take a look at you."

Tracy wished she had taken time to change into a clean shirt at least. She walked over and looked down at the woman in the wheelchair. Tracy remembered her father or Miss Story or someone referring to the woman as Big Bertha. She was big, probably even bigger than they remembered. She seemed to overflow the wheelchair, but you could tell her bigness had once been muscle rather than fat, and even sitting down she seemed tall. Her face was not fat at all, but it was big: the nose, the high forehead, the eyes, the jaw.

She put on a pair of steel-rimmed glasses and peered at Tracy for several unnerving moments. "You look like her," she said finally.

"That's what Miss Story said."

"She did, did she? Is she the one told you who your mother was?"

"No, my parents told me. After we moved here. They said my . . . my mother didn't want them to tell me until after she died."

"That's right. I guess I was the only one, outside of your parents, of course, who knew the story." Her voice was deep, and after the first few minutes she looked away from Tracy, as if looking into the past. "I was the one suggested Jackie Stewart. She wanted somebody steady, and I said you couldn't find a steadier boy than Jackie." She paused. "That screwball she married, he ran out on her, you know, and she hadn't even told him she was pregnant. I told her that that marriage wouldn't work, and it didn't. Both of them hung up on their great careers. . . ." She sniffed scornfully. "Two big egos. She worked right up till the last three months. You couldn't tell she was pregnant unless you had sharp eyes. She told her agent she was going to the country for a long rest, and he told the club owners she was on a European tour. Didn't do her any harm, that didn't. When she came back and needed a job, the tales she had to tell! About her triumphs in London and Paris and all over. I guess her agent knew good and well what she'd been up to, but he played along, it was money in his pocket. Felicia never made the big time, but she did all right. Chicago, Las Vegas, Reno, places like that. They'd get her to sing in their cocktail lounges. Never been to those places myself, but I guess they have somebody play the piano or guitar and sing while everybody sits around getting drunk in the afternoon." She stopped, and was silent for so long that Tracy began to think she had finished.

"Why didn't she have an abortion?" Tracy said. It was something she had wondered about a lot.

"Too expensive in those days, and she wasn't sure it was the right thing to do. So there we were, both of us up a crick. My husband had drowned off the Georges Bank. . . ."

"He was a fisherman?" Tracy thought of the wreaths floating in Gloucester harbor.

"What else? You don't go to Georges Bank for the view. So I was stuck with Rosie, two years old, and her brother, five. I had this ramshackle old cottage on a lake near Portsmouth, New Hampshire, that my grandmother left me. I said to Felicia, Let's go up there till things settle down. So we did."

"I was born in New Hampshire?"

"I just said so."

No, you didn't, Tracy thought, but she didn't say it.

"Lake Pleasant, but it wasn't. I had to row to town for groceries and all. The last week we got this midwife to move in with us. She didn't care much for the place, but she stuck it out until you were born. Then she hightailed it out of there. Charged Felicia twice what she'd said. Wasn't used to such a primitive place, she said." Again she was silent, absently fiddling with a small package on the table.

"Then what?" Tracy said.

"Well, Felicia had already made arrangements with Jackie and his wife. The wife had a hard time with the first baby and she wasn't in any rush to have another, but they wanted a second child."

Then I *was* wanted, Tracy thought; it wasn't some kind of favor they did for Felicia.

"So we shut up the cabin and rowed into town. Jackie showed up with his wife and they took the baby. You." She looked at Tracy as if she had forgotten that was who she was talking about. "Felicia flew out to Vegas, and I come back here to the old homestead, and here I am to this day." She sounded bitter.

"Why did my mother want it kept a secret all her life?"

"Oh, she couldn't stand kids. Didn't want one showing up someday and making things awkward. Felicia hated responsibility. The only thing she was ever responsible about was her career. Never missed a rehearsal, never missed a performance. Or so she said, and I believe it. She'd had the baby and she wanted to forget the whole thing."

Tracy shivered.

"When she got lung cancer from all those cigarettes she smoked, she moved to someplace in New Mexico . . . where was it now?"

"Santa Fe."

"That's it. Said the air was clearer or something, as if air could cure lung cancer. Anyway, right there near the end she sent me this." She shook open the envelope she had been fiddling with. Her hands were twisted with arthritis and for a moment she couldn't get the envelope open. Then a cassette tape fell out. She shoved it across the table to Tracy. "Said I was to give it to you. I don't know what's in it. We don't have any of those fancy players, so I couldn't listen even if I wanted to, and I don't." She leaned back in her chair. "So there you are. That's my story. Now I'm tired, so I thank you for coming over, and I'll say goodbye. You're in good hands with Jackie and his wife. You're lucky. God knows what would have become of you if Felicia had tried to keep you. Not that she'd ever have dreamed of it."

"Can I ask you one question?" Tracy held the tape in her hand.

"Fire away."

"Did you like my mother?"

"Well, sure. We were first cousins, and we were friends all our lives. She was wild as a sea gull and just as tough, and you can see for yourself I'm not wild. . . ."

"But I think you're tough," Tracy said. "I admire that."

The woman gave a hoarse chuckle. "You do, do you? My Rose says you and she are friends."

"Yes, we are."

"Well, she can use one. You be nice to her." She closed her eyes.

"Thank you," Tracy whispered. She went out quietly, making sure not to let any flies in.

Chapter 22

❖ ❖ ❖

Tracy closed her bedroom door and put the tape in her cassette player. She hesitated, almost scared to press the START button.

For a few seconds the tape whirred. Then a deep, slightly hoarse voice said, "Well, where do I start? This is Felicia Shaw, and it so happens I'm your mother. It also so happens I'll be sailing off into the wide blue yonder by the time you hear this. Dead, in other words. It makes me mad, but it doesn't scare me. I mean, it happens to everybody, right? Only it's a little sooner than I'd planned on." There was a pause. "I guess Bertha's given you the bare facts. I asked her to. So I'll skip the vital statistics and all that jazz. I just wanted to tell you it was nothing personal, my not keeping you. I just can't stand kids. I said in the agreement to tell you when you were eighteen. If you wanted to look me up then, we could chance it. You'd be more or less grown-up. I wouldn't have to wrap you in a diaper and hide you in the dressing room, right? And we might even like each other. Sometimes when I heard Judy and Liza, I thought, Hey, wouldn't it be neat . . . But who knows, you may be Johnny-one-note."

"I am," Tracy murmured.

"If you wonder about your old man, don't bother. El Creepo, that one. I always did leap before I looked. I had a lot of much better guys hanging around, but I never was a good chooser. Listen, if you ever run into a fella named Horace Webster, tell him I'm sorry about that pail of water in his face." She stopped, laughed, and coughed for several seconds. "But it *was* funny. Bertha has a scrapbook with all my clippings, pictures and stuff, if you want to see it. I looked pretty good, I don't mind saying, before this damned cancer hit me. I was always vain as a peacock. Now I won't look in the mirror. Ah, well, as the song goes, 'Laugh it off, laugh it off, laugh it off.' I hope you can laugh at life, kiddo. It's the only thing that saves you." She paused. "They'll tell you I was a wild kid. You bet. Wild all the way and loved every minute of it. I thought you might like to hear how I sounded, before all this crap hit me, so I'm going to put a couple of songs off other tapes onto this one. If I can find the right buttons. I hate machines. Hang in there a minute."

After a few seconds she came on again, coughing. "Listen, be smart—don't smoke. Anyway, here goes with a couple songs I did up at Lake Tahoe last year. The first one is a silly little folk song they used to like. Kind of fun. Hold your hat—here we go."

The song started. It was a lively, funny song that began, "Beware, young ladies, they're fooling you, they're fooling you, they're fooling you. Beware, young ladies, they're fooling you, beware, oh, beware." Felicia's voice sounded strong and husky, and without the hoarseness. She played a fast, skillful guitar.

Her voice came on again when it ended. "Did it make you smile?"

"Yes," Tracy said softly.

"Here's a ballad coming up, nice and sobby and sentimental. Grab your hankie."

Tracy thought she had heard it before. Part of it went: "The party's over—the candles flicker and dim. . . ." It was pretty, but it made her feel sad.

"All right, one more for the road," Felicia said. "I have a nerve singing this one when Cleo Laine does it so superbly, but nerve is what I've got plenty of."

It was a song Tracy had heard Alison play on her tape deck, by Sondheim. It had a jaunty, defiant refrain that went, "But I'm still *here*."

"Enough already," Felicia's voice said. "I won't be 'here' when you play this, but I'm here now, and who knows what next? I was never scared of risks. Remember to take risks, Daughter. Never let life be dull, and you'll be okay. It's weird talking to you. I've thought a lot about—"

The snap of the tape shutting off made Tracy jump. She turned it over and punched PLAY, but there was only the faint hum of the tape winding. There was nothing on it. What had Felicia been going to say? Tracy was glad she had called her "Daughter."

I like her, she thought. She had guts and she could laugh. So she was irresponsible sometimes. Nobody's perfect. She started when Alison knocked on the door.

"I've just come from Deland's," she said. "David is beginning to look not quite so stricken. Miss Story took him to Ipswich and bought him some clothes and some of the things he lost in the fire, the replaceable things." She shook her head. "But he's lost so much, Trace, like losing his life almost. I feel so sorry for him. But people have been wonderful. All kinds of presents, and people stopping by to say how sorry they are. This is really a good town, you know it?"

"Yes, it is." Tracy felt a pang of guilt for having temporarily forgotten David. The tape had made her forget everything. "What can I do for him?"

"He and Miss Story are coming here for dinner. Try to make him smile. He needs to smile. He likes you a lot, Trace." She glanced at the tape deck. "What have you been listening to?"

Tracy put the tape in her bureau drawer. "Tell you later." Someday she would play it for Alison, no one else. "Who are Judy and Liza?"

"Garland and Minnelli. Why?"

Tracy shook her head and followed Alison downstairs, smiling at the notion of herself as Liza Minnelli, she who couldn't carry a tune to the woodshed, as her father said.

"How was it with Rosie's mother?"

"Okay. It's a long story. I'll tell you later."

Tracy went downstairs into the noise and confusion of her family, smelling onions and mushrooms sautéing in butter. It would be nice to have David and Miss Story with them tonight. Maybe she could help David to understand that even if your real family isn't there, friends can be a kind of family too.

DATE DUE

FOLLETT